Deanna stared in disb____ _____
screen:

I am seeking a young man named Aaron Walker. He just turned twenty-two. He comes from the West Coast—Washington State to be exact—a small town called Oysterville. Aaron knows a lot about oysters, as his father is an oysterman. He might mention having three older brothers and a sister who died of cystic fibrosis.

He is medium height, has sandy blond hair, and is a friendly sort. If you have any info, please contact me at this E-mail address.

Deanna felt fear rush over her. Fear like she always felt when she thought Aaron might move on. This Courtney had to be an old girlfriend. How else would she know this much about him?

BIRDIE L. ETCHISON lives in Washington State and knows much about the Pacific Northwest, the setting for the majority of her books. She loves to research the colorful history of the United States and uses her research along with family stories to create wonderful novels.

Books by Birdie L. Etchison

HEARTSONG PRESENTS

Don't miss out on any of our super romances. Write to us at the following address for information on our newest releases and club membership.

Heartsong Presents Readers' Service
PO Box 721
Uhrichsville, OH 44683

Or visit www.heartsongpresents.com

Ring
of Hope

Birdie L. Etchison

Heartsong Presents

To Ashley, Aurora, Tianna, and Isaac—
four bright stars in my life

A note from the author:
I love to hear from my readers! You may correspond with me
by writing:

> **Birdie L. Etchison**
> **Author Relations**
> **PO Box 719**
> **Uhrichsville, OH 44683**

ISBN 1-58660-595-X

RING OF HOPE

All Scripture quotations are taken from King James Version of the
Bible.

All of the characters and events in this book are fictitious. Any
resemblance to actual persons, living or dead, or to actual events
is purely coincidental.

Cover design by Jocelyne Bouchard.

PRINTED IN THE U.S.A.

one

East Belfast, Maine

Deanna Barnes was preparing the Lobster Pound, an outdoor fresh-lobster restaurant, for the evening's festivities. A birthday party for twelve was scheduled, and GB, her brother, had reluctantly agreed to stay to help. Her daughter Madison clutched at her coat, looking up at Deanna with her dark brown eyes.

"You know, my part of the job ends when I bring in the day's catch." GB turned the water on under the lobster pots. "Maybe Dad should hire someone."

Deanna shrugged. "I suggested an ad in the local paper, but Dad doesn't want to. He thinks someone will just come walking up looking for work."

"Maybe they will. He's been right before."

Their father, Mick, entered the room, as if he knew they were talking about him. "I've been praying for someone to come by and give us a hand around here. I think my prayers will be answered soon."

Mick, a grizzled old man with a head full of gray hair and a short beard, owned the Lobster Pound. He did the buying, hiring, and firing, and his word was the final say. He nodded now, looking from son to daughter, then granddaughter.

"Of course we'll manage," Deanna said with a smile. "We always seem to get by somehow." She hugged her father, hard. He sounded gruff, but there wasn't an unkind bone in his body. "We could advertise and have more parties if we had help; that's all I was thinking about."

5

"Help is coming." He stuck a cherry-wood pipe in his mouth and chewed on the end. He never lit it, but it was his comfort, his pacifier.

"Madison, you must sit at your little desk now and color or draw pictures. Mommy is going to be very, very busy."

"And I'll just get in the way?"

"Yes, Honey. That's about it." Deanna had to look away, not wanting to see the girl's expression, her strong chin—both so like her father's. If only Bobby had lived. They would have all the help they needed. Who knew, when he'd gone to check the traps that afternoon, that a nor'easter would blow up? Storms were capricious here in Maine, and that had been a bad one.

The boiling pots were nearly ready; Deanna set out plates and silverware with tubs of butter and thick slabs of French bread. The tables and benches on the upper floor, where people ate their lobster, were clean, but she hadn't finished the floor and was ashamed that it had only been swept and not mopped. A sign overhead listed menu items, including crab, mussels, haddock, halibut, cod, and scallops.

She didn't hear the car, but GB did. "Someone just drove in. Maybe it's Dad's answer to prayer."

Deanna looked up. Soon the parking lot would be full. "Why do you say that? It's probably just an early customer."

"Just a hunch."

Their father had walked up the hill and was talking to a man who stood near a car that was a rust bucket if she'd ever seen one. The man was young looking, which meant he would be strong and full of energy. The two came down the hill, her father leaning on his cane, the younger man walking with a spring in his step.

"This is Aaron," Mick said, nodding toward the sandy-haired man. "He's looking for work. Do you think we could use him for a few days? Told him I hadn't gotten around to advertising. If it weren't for this ol' rheumatism, I'd be doing more. . . ."

Deanna looked up into the stranger's eyes and felt a sudden pang at his steady gaze. A person could tell so much from a person's eyes. She held out her hand. "I'm Deanna. Nice to meet you, Aaron."

"And you."

He wasn't from around here; she was almost positive. Just two words spoken, but she hadn't detected a Maine accent.

"This is GB, my brother, and my daughter, Madison."

"Maddy!" the little girl proclaimed.

"Maddy for short," Deanna said with a nod.

A bark sounded as a huge black lab bounded around the side of the Pound and stopped alongside Aaron. He sniffed Aaron's shoes, but the hair didn't go up on his back.

"Murphy here thinks he owns the place. He's anything but a watchdog and can't stand to be left out of a thing." He nuzzled Aaron's hand when he stopped patting the big dog's head.

"Yeah, I'd say you passed muster," Mick said.

"Where are you from?" GB asked, a frown creasing his brow.

"Been around." Aaron smiled. "Was working the forest, logging trees and sending them off down the Kennebec. Worked in a toothpick factory before that, and then in June I decided to hike the Appalachian Trail."

GB turned and listened now.

"Made it to Mt. Katahdin," Aaron continued, "then back to this logging area."

"A logger and a hiker?" GB looked almost impressed—or about as impressed as he ever would look.

Deanna figured that explained the hiking boots, denims, and well-worn backpack. Still, she didn't think he was from Maine—not born and bred.

"Been wanting to do something else," Aaron said, shifting his gaze back to Deanna. "I like the water. I want to find work on a lobster boat."

"You have a license?" she asked.

"No." There was a slight hesitation.

GB crossed his arms. "Well, you must have a license to run a boat around here. And I already have a sternman so I don't need anyone to help on the boat just now."

Another puzzlement, Deanna thought. If Aaron were from Maine, he'd know about restrictions for lobstermen.

"Sternman." Aaron repeated the word.

"You know. The one who baits the traps. Sis used to do it, but then she got married."

"You don't need help with the boat, GB; but we do need someone to help out here with the Pound," Deanna quickly added.

"Yeah, that we do." GB, a younger version of his father, frowned. "Say, I wanted to hike the Appalachian Trail but never got around to it. Where does it start?"

Aaron looked cautious, as if he knew he was being questioned for a reason. "Springer Mountain in northern Georgia. We can talk about it sometime, if you like."

Mick seemed oblivious to the conversation while Deanna continued to study the young man who had appeared, it seemed, in answer to her silent prayer.

"Deanna can show you what to do," said GB. "You decide. Stay and work here or move on. After one night of work, you'll have your answer." GB tossed his white apron into a bin in a corner of the room.

Deanna nodded. "That I can do. Been working the Pound a long while now. I could boil lobster in my sleep."

She realized that Aaron might be a logger, and that was fine and good, but he didn't know about lobstering. He couldn't fool her; he had come from somewhere else. Not that it mattered. They needed help, and if this was the one whom the good Lord had sent, then it would work.

Deanna pointed to the holding tank. Several lobsters of various sizes swam in the water. "People come here first, select the lobster they want. Someone, and I guess that could be you now, takes the lobster out with the net here, then dumps it in the pot."

"How long does it take to cook?" Aaron asked.

"It varies. I'll show you what to do, how to test the lobster."

"Okay. I think I can manage that."

"Dad weighs the lobster, takes the money, and I get the plates ready, slice the bread, and melt butter for the lobster."

"But where do the customers eat?"

Deanna pointed. "The tables are all upstairs. You'll be running up and down these stairs all night. Guess it's good that you're a hiker. Otherwise, you probably couldn't do it."

She knew he was watching her as she started up the steps with a tray of napkins and silverware. Aaron carried another tray with supplies, which included a package of balloons.

The tables were picnic style, painted white with benches to match. The floor was wide, unpainted planks, with a view of the river. The Pound looked like a dock, tied down on the rocks at tide line. Several boats bobbed up and down in the harbor, with one heading in now.

"We get customers who come in on boats, tie up at the dock, and come over. Others arrive in cars. Tonight we're having a party, so if you want to blow up some balloons and tack them to the posts, that would help."

Deanna wished he would quit staring at her. He looked young, too young for her—if she was interested, which she was not. She had loved Bobby with all her heart and had no intention to marry again. At least not for awhile.

"How long is the Pound open?"

"Most of the year, unless we have a severe winter. Our regular customers stop by for lobster, and we also do mail order."

"Uh-huh."

"Mommy!" Maddy's voice called from below. "Can I come up there?"

"No, Honey. We're heading down."

Aaron followed her down the wide, deep steps, and she knew he was staring at her again.

"Do you think this is something you want to do?"

He nodded. "I like to learn new things, and as I said before, I've always loved the water."

"And where did you grow up?" She felt she had to ask.

"Does that matter? Do I not get the job if you don't know that?"

"You're not from Maine," she said, avoiding his steady gaze.

"No, I'm not. But I've lived here going on four years now."

"I see."

Mick walked over, holding his granddaughter's hand. "So, what do you think of the place?"

"It's good." Aaron looked at the older man again. "I think I can handle the job."

"I 'spect you'll need a place to stay," Mick said.

"Well, Sir, I do at that."

"The Seaview Cottage is down the road a piece," Mick said. "You're welcome to stay there for a bit."

"Dad!" The word escaped from Deanna's mouth before she could stop it. Her face turned red.

"What? Why not let him stay in the cottage? Been sitting there vacant long enough!" His tone was gruff, but Aaron just smiled.

"Oh." She looked at Aaron again and pulled back her dark, thick hair, then reached for a hair net. Her father was right, as always, but it was hard to think of someone sitting at the kitchen table or nestling in the bed. . . .

"Been sleeping in your car, I bet."

Aaron nodded. "Yeah, I have."

"You can help out tonight, then my daughter will have you

sign a contract for the cottage—"

"I have no money," Aaron said. "That is, I won't until I've worked a few days."

Mick turned, took his hat off, and put it back on again, eyeing Aaron all the while. "I somehow knew that, young man, but you can pay me the end of next week."

Deanna felt like saying more but realized it was time to get busy.

Aaron watched while Deanna picked out a lobster, as if she were choosing that one for her dinner. "Now you do it."

He caught the live lobster from the tank, using a wooden trap that set down inside the water. "Why do their claws have rubber bands on them?" he asked.

"Because they're cannibals," Mick said with a laugh. "They'd eat one another if we didn't keep them banded."

Then Deanna showed him how to cook one by dropping it into the pot of boiling water, then testing to see if it was done. "We throw them in alive; that's so people know that they are fresh."

"Seems kind of cruel."

"It is, but their misery is short-lived. Here now, watch. If you cook a lobster too long, they're tough. Meat's stringy. People won't be back if you don't serve good lobster." She gave Aaron a puzzled look. "A lot of our customers are tourists, you know." She stood back, as if surveying the situation. "I think you should just wait on customers tonight."

"Okay. Whatever."

Aaron blew up the balloons and made three trips up the stairs with butter, extra plates, and ashtrays. Since it was an open-air restaurant, people could smoke. Dress was casual. Aaron's first customers were from Pennsylvania.

"We saw the Lobster Pound sign from Highway One."

Aaron grinned. "That's what brought me here too. This is my first night working here."

Another birthday party came, and Deanna watched while Aaron ran up and down the steps. He might feel it in his legs in the morning, but being a hiker, perhaps not. She wondered what it would be like to hike along for miles and miles. Not that she could ever hope to do that, not now that she had Maddy.

At last it was nine o'clock, and she turned off the OPEN sign.

"I'll like working here," Aaron said as Maddy peered out from around her mother's legs.

"You'll be busy, that's for sure," Deanna answered, turning to go behind the counter.

Aaron tossed his apron into the bin along with GB's. "I suppose I better start the cleanup."

"Don't you worry about the upstairs," Mick answered. "Plenty of time to get at it tomorrow."

"Are you sure?"

"Yup."

Deanna removed her hair net, letting the curls bounce as she walked.

"I like your hair," he said, and then his face reddened.

She felt her face flush too as she handed him a clipboard and a pen. "Thank you," she murmured. "This is the form Dad talked about. Just says that you will leave everything as it is now." Her eyes met his again. "It's pretty standard." She looked away.

Murphy came from around the side of the Lobster Barn, went up to Aaron, and pushed against his hand, wanting attention again. Aaron bent down and nuzzled the dog, then made a face. "You're wet!"

"He loves the water. All labs do. Bet someone threw a stick for him to fetch," Mick said.

"How long you staying?" Deanna asked.

"A few months, probably."

One dark eyebrow arched. "Then moving on?"

"Maybe longer. It all depends."

Deanna got that quivery feeling inside again. She didn't want to feel this way. Bobby had been gone only a little over a year.

"Here's the key. No need for me to go with you. The linens are in the closet just outside the bathroom door, and there are dishes and extra blankets in a cedar chest at the foot of the bed."

Aaron took the key, his hand touching hers briefly. "There's only one problem," he said. "Your father pointed north, but I don't see anything. You didn't give me directions."

"Just follow the path. It's around two bends, hidden in some trees. Can't miss it."

"I'll see you in the morning then."

She hesitated before answering. "You could. . .come up to the main house for a bite to eat. I know it's late, but we get too busy to eat until now. Our main meal's at noon."

He frowned, as if thinking it over. "I'm kinda tired. Think I'll just unpack, shower, and go to bed. Thanks anyway."

Deanna watched while he walked up the hill to his car, hoisting a large duffel bag over his shoulder, then took off in the direction she'd pointed. A knot rose in her chest. She hadn't been inside the cottage for a long time, and she wondered if Aaron would find it to his liking. There were so many memories there. . . .

Murphy bounded down the path after him, but Aaron turned and pointed in the direction of the Pound. Her father was right. Murphy, as most dogs, was a good judge of character, and he definitely approved of the new worker. Deanna took Maddy's hand and headed toward the house.

two

Aaron knew Deanna was watching him. He had wanted to ask why it mattered if he rented the cottage. Those brown eyes of hers concealed secrets. She had the child, so she must be married, but where was her husband? Away at sea? In the service? Maybe he'd find out later, but perhaps not. You couldn't tell about these people from Maine. They seemed to lock their hearts inside, not sharing with anyone.

He didn't want to think of how tired he was right now. Exhausted. And hungry. But soon he'd sleep in a real bed and hear the water lapping against the shore.

Aaron could hardly believe his good luck, but it had been like that since he'd first left his home five years ago. Jobs were offered him at the precise moment he was down to his last dollar. More often than not, he had a roof over his head. He'd known when he hit Belfast and saw the Lobster Pound sign that he would stop to see if they could use an extra hand. He'd worked on crab boats back in Oysterville. He loved the water. He knew the water, and the Lobster Pound sat at the edge of the river, which flowed into Penabscot Bay. This was perfect.

Aaron made his way down the path that wound around and through a copse of pine and birch.

And then he saw it. A weather-beaten cottage, small and cozy as he had expected, was built into the hill, with briars and brambles creeping up one side. He made his way through a tangle of spider webs, opened the door, and stepped in.

He dropped his duffel bag just inside the door. He'd get the trunk out of his car later. A round braided rug decorated the

14

linoleum floor. The couch looked comfortable, and a small TV sat under the window hung with red floral curtains. Someone had lived here. That someone had made it look pleasant. It had to have been Deanna. She must have been married, because her last name was different from her dad's. The little girl, a tiny replica of her mother, had her mother's dancing, dark curls. Tonight he had wanted to touch Deanna's curls, but of course he had not.

Aaron opened the cupboard. There were pots, pans, dishes, silverware, more than he'd ever need. This would do just fine.

Behind a drawn curtain was a double bed. A quilt with a bright red tulip design covered the bed, a four-poster. He would put the duffel in the closet and unpack tomorrow.

He sat on the edge of the bed and removed his boots. He couldn't explain it, but somehow he felt as if he'd come home. It was strange, but after only a few hours, Deanna had caused him to grow introspective, to consider that maybe it was time to think about settling down. Yet, why wouldn't that settling place be Oysterville? Had it really been five years since he'd left on that cold, windy October morning?

&

All night long, Hannah had coughed. The cough was worse this night than most times. Aaron had sat huddled on his bed, listening and knowing that his little sister was dying. Nobody wanted to admit it. Cora, their part-time housekeeper who had taken over after an aunt died, said, "She'll be okay in a week or so." And his father wouldn't discuss it at all. He'd go pound her on the back and take her to yet another doctor. The diagnosis was always the same. People with cystic fibrosis do not live a full life.

Aaron remembered Hannah's good days. Hannah with her big, big smile—the little girl he had loved more than anyone. They'd spent summers digging for clams, going with their father to check crab pots. There'd been hikes out to Leadbetter

Point. When she could no longer walk to the road to catch the school bus, Leighton Walker had paid a tutor to come teach her math and English, the two subjects he deemed most important.

Aaron had gotten out of bed that last night and offered to make his father a cup of coffee, but his father had pushed the idea aside, moving past Aaron as he headed for Hannah's bedroom.

"Just go away, Aaron. There's nothing you can do!"

It had been true, of course. Aaron knew that, but if only his father had hugged him or looked at him as if he cared. But he hadn't, and Aaron went back to his room and thought about the plans he'd made a few weeks earlier. It was time to go. He made his bed, cleaned off the top of his dresser, and stuffed as many clothes as he could into the duffel bag. The Bible Grandma had given him was put in the bottom, along with a small photo album of family pictures.

The first traces of dawn were creeping over the Willapa Hills and casting shadows across the bay when Aaron slung the bag over his shoulder and headed out. And he didn't look back. Nor had he ever looked back since leaving Oysterville that morning.

Now, as Aaron lay across the bed in the small, neat cottage of his employer, he wondered if he'd ever stop feeling guilty about running off like that. He should have left a note, but he hadn't even done that. He'd had no idea of where he'd go. Seventeen, a year left of school, and a runaway.

It wasn't as if Hannah was the only family. There were three older brothers, Thomas, Luke, and John. But they had never been close, and he'd always just been the "little brother." Sometimes he talked to Luke, but then Luke married and was too busy to stop by.

Aaron opened his eyes and thought of Deanna again, how loving she was to her child and to her father and brother. The family was tight. He'd never known that feeling. Aaron's mother had left because she couldn't handle the role of mothering an extremely sick child. Later, she committed suicide in Seattle. He always wondered if he couldn't have done something, maybe tell her he loved her, and then perhaps she wouldn't have killed herself. The last time he'd seen her was when she waited outside his first-grade classroom and then took him out for an ice cream cone. If only he'd known. . .

He couldn't sleep, so got up, found his food stash and ate the last of the potato chips, then he looked to see if there was anything in the cupboards. A can of cinnamon, a box of soda, an old jar of instant coffee that had dried up at the bottom, and a package of assorted teas were on a top shelf. Five bags were left, so he put water on for tea. He much preferred coffee, but tea would suffice. He chose peppermint, and soon the smell filled the cottage. At least the cup kept his hands warm as he thought of the dark curls and the brown eyes. Again he wondered why she seemed protective of the cabin. Her sharp intake of breath happened when her father asked if he wanted to use the cottage.

Aaron rinsed the cup and went to the bedroom. Maybe he should just go ahead and unpack. Why wait? He opened the closet and saw a dress hanging at one end. Deanna's wedding gown. This had been Deanna and her groom's home; he was sure of that. It was her love he felt when he first stepped inside—a pleasant ambiance that soothed him. It had her touch. And he felt her presence. He knew she must be older; he had turned twenty-two just last week but felt much older and wiser than when he ran off.

Aaron turned on a small radio and listened to a soft-rock station. He had to sleep, as he was expected to work early. Fishermen never slept in, and neither would he. Tomorrow would be here before he was ready.

&

"Dad?" Deanna stepped into the living room. The TV was

silent, but she could hear her father's gruff voice reading a book to Maddy.

"We're upstairs, Mommy. Grandpa's reading *The Cat in the Hat*."

"Okay, Honey." *Weird,* Deanna thought. Usually her father would have a cup of coffee and the TV on, with Maddy playing house or making a fort for her plush animals.

Deanna opened the refrigerator and took out sandwich meat. They ate their big meal at noon, so the evening was usually a snack. Her thoughts went to Aaron again. No one since Bobby had made her heart pound like this, and thinking about Aaron now made it race again. *Silly,* she admonished herself. *You know nothing about him.* And that was what seemed so strange about her father inviting him to stay in the Seaview cottage. *How could he?* she asked herself again. The man could be an escaped convict, someone who might rob them. The money taken in each night was fairly accessible; they'd never been worried about robbery before.

She chewed her lip, a nervous habit she couldn't control, as she set the pan on the stove. Funny that she'd think that about him. He definitely did not look the dangerous type. In fact, she was certain he was younger than she was. He had a little-boy quality about him that appealed to her father, but it was the depth, the loneliness in his eyes, that spoke to her heart.

Deanna put sandwiches on the table and microwaved a cup of coffee. "Hey, you two," she called up the stairs. "Wanna eat a bite?" She smiled as she heard the scuffling of feet on the floor and their affirmative answer.

Her father entered the kitchen first, with Maddy close behind. Deanna thought it the perfect moment to voice her reservations about Aaron.

"Dad, about the new help. . ."

"Now don't go a-gettin' mad at me." He pulled his chair out. "I know it was an impulsive thing to do, giving Aaron the Seaview Cottage, but it was as if God was nudging me, saying, 'Here is your worker. Trust me. He's a good kid.' "

"Who's a kid?" Maddy asked, tilting her head.

"You are!" her grandfather said, pretending he'd nipped her nose off her face. "See, I got it right here!"

"You don't either, Grandpa! It's still here!" Then she started giggling.

After the blessing and she'd taken two bites of her sandwich, Deanna looked up. "Dad, I know we needed someone desperately, and I know God works in mysterious ways, but to offer him the cottage. . . Why, I haven't even—"

"What? Cleaned it out? It looks just fine to me and is going to look like a palace to a kid who's been working in the woods and living in his car. He's an honest one, Deanna."

"I like that man who worked for us today. . . ," Maddy said.

"Aaron," her mother said. "His name is Aaron."

"Ae-won."

"No. Air-un. You can say air, like the air you breathe, Maddy."

"Aaron!" she shouted.

"Yes," Deanna said. "Now eat your sandwich." Deanna wasn't too worried if her daughter didn't eat well now, because she always had food at the Pound for Maddy to eat.

Deanna looked at her father. "I invited him to eat with us," she volunteered.

"So, you must think he's okay. Just don't want to admit it."

"Oh, Dad. It just surprised me. You know I've tried to go down there and take things out, but it's just too hard."

"Are there any cookies?" Mick asked, as if wanting to change the subject.

"Does a bear live in the woods?"

She poured a glass of milk, put two sugar cookies on a plate, and took them over to the recliner. "Here you go."

Turning toward Maddy, she said, "And you, young miss,

need a bath before bedtime."

After Mick had gone on to bed and Maddy was sound asleep, Deanna sat in the living room. She liked sitting in the dark among the late evening shadows. As long as she could remember, the dark, whether it was morning or night, held a fascination for her. She could talk things over with God.

Tonight, her thoughts kept going to Aaron and where he was now. The cottage had been her home for two years. She'd sewn floral curtains for the kitchen, made pillows for the living room, and cross-stitched a Maine sunrise. The bedroom walls were painted blue because it was Bobby's favorite color. "The color of a summer sky," he'd once said, pulling her close that first night in their new home. And now Aaron would have that bedroom. In the closet he'd find her white satin gown wrapped in layers of plastic. There was no way he'd miss the dress.

Why was her mind wandering, thinking, dreaming? Her heart had pounded at the sight of the young man, but she admonished herself for even thinking that some day there might be another man, a soul mate. Yet she sensed Aaron was going to mean something to her life. She wasn't sure how she knew; she just did. A verse, Psalm 44:21, went through her mind: *"He knoweth the secrets of the heart."* She believed that with her whole heart and deep down knew that God often answered prayers in surprising ways.

Deanna thought of when she'd met Bobby and how fast they had fallen in love. They were young, "too young to marry," her father had said, but they married anyway. Four years of marriage, a child born that first year, and now a year since Bobby's death. It had been one of the worst "sneaker storms" to hit the Atlantic Coast, and he had asked her to go out with him to check the traps. Sometimes she wished she had, but then Madison wouldn't have had either parent.

She made Bobby a saint after he died, but she knew there

had been a hint of unraveling in their relationship. He had not shared her faith, her love of God—and marriage meant being equally yoked. It also meant giving and taking.

She shook the thoughts from her mind. Maybe it was time to stop mourning Bobby's death, to move on; perhaps she could once again make a home for a man who would love her in return. Yet Aaron couldn't be that man. He was a drifter, a wanderer. She didn't want that. She had to keep reminding herself that physical attraction was not important—there were spiritual aspects to a marriage that really counted. God would direct her to the right person. Some day.

three

Deanna rose at four as she always did this time of year. Usually she was rested and ready to meet the day, but just knowing that someone was in the Seaview Cottage made her night restless. Her father was right. It didn't make sense to leave the cottage empty. It should be used.

She filled the coffee pot. Her father expected his morning coffee, crisp bacon, scrambled eggs, and several thick slices of toast for breakfast. And there was always a pot of oatmeal. She could do this in her sleep. Thank goodness Maddy was still in bed and would not get up for another hour. These few minutes gave Deanna an opportunity to mull over the day and to have morning devotions. When her mother was alive, they would sit together at the oak table, hold hands, and pray for each other before their day unfolded. How she missed that. More than anything, she'd dreamed of running her home that way too.

She pulled her hair back and tied it with a red ribbon to match her shirt. The dark curls sprang in ringlets, still damp from her shower. Aaron had noticed her hair. Silly. Here she was again, thinking of him. She set the slices of homemade bread aside, turned the coffee on low, and sat at the table, her head bent over her Bible. She read Proverbs 10:22: "The blessing of the Lord, it maketh rich, and he addeth no sorrow with it." Deanna jotted down a few thoughts in her journal: *"Patience, Lord—You know I need patience. Let me be happy with the blessings of my child, a father I adore, and a brother who causes me problems but is still my brother."*

❧

Aaron got up before dawn, found the granola bars in his duffel and the last container of orange juice. He gulped it down and then showered. He donned his heaviest pair of jeans, a T-shirt, a red flannel, heavy socks, and boots. When he stepped outside and felt the fresh, crisp air, he grabbed his stocking cap and pulled it down over his ears. Mornings were usually brisk on the water. Maybe he'd let his hair grow out, as he had last winter. He might even try a beard. He had planned walking along the water, but when he saw the light in the bigger house, he headed toward it.

He paused before knocking, hoping he wouldn't disturb anyone. Deanna answered the door, and his heart caught in his throat.

"I wouldn't have come, but I saw the light. Forgive me if I've intruded."

"I'm surprised you're up this early. But do come in! Why not have a cup of coffee and eat breakfast with us?"

"Oh, no. I just wondered if I should go down to the Pound and begin cleaning up from last night."

"Before breakfast?" Her eyes met his, but only for a moment.

"I've eaten."

"Oh." She looked disappointed.

The Bible lay open on the table. "You were reading, and I interrupted."

Deanna smiled as she closed her Bible. "Morning devotions," she said, as if she needed to explain. "I was reading Proverbs. It gives so many rules for life. Are you a believer, by chance?"

Aaron paused. "I—well—yes, I believe."

She wondered if he was just saying that for her benefit; yet there was a certain longing in his eyes as he looked at the Bible, as if remembering a time when he'd read the Scriptures.

A shuffling noise sounded on the stairway, and moments later Mick entered the room. "Ah, the new worker. More than punctual, eh?" He stroked his beard and looked from Deanna to Aaron. "Throw a couple more eggs in."

"No, Sir, I've eaten. I just wanted to get started cleaning the upstairs, or whatever it is you want me to do."

"Mommy!" a tiny voice called from the top of the stairs. "Can I get up yet?"

"Of course. Come on down. The oatmeal's ready."

"But I want Cap'n Crunch."

"Whatever." She looked over at Aaron. "Usually she sleeps longer, but it isn't every morning that two deep, baritone voices fill the house."

The little girl in a flannel nightgown and Donald Duck slippers soon wrapped her arms around her mother's legs and held on for dear life.

"Hi, Maddy!" Aaron held out his hand. "I'm sorry if I woke you up."

"No." She rubbed her eyes. "It was Grandpa."

"I sound like a foghorn, that's for sure," the older man bellowed.

She ran over and threw her arms around him. "I like your voice, Grandpa."

"I insist you sit with us; have a cup of coffee and at least some of Deanna's toast." Mick poured two mugs of coffee and set them on the table. "We have simple fare, but it's plenty and filling."

Aaron sipped his coffee, while Mick added cream and sugar. He offered them to Aaron. "No, it's strong, just the way I like it. And hot."

The older man talked while Deanna flitted back and forth from counter to stove, from refrigerator to stove. In moments she had tomato juice on the table, three plates, and two bowls. Bacon sizzled in a skillet, while she cracked eggs into a small bowl and whisked them. She could feel Aaron watching her, and she wondered what he was thinking. He certainly wasn't talkative like her father, and Maine people were known to be reserved. Not Mick Nelson's family.

Maddy slipped off her grandfather's lap after one small sip of his coffee and sat at the far end of the table on a booster chair.

"Maddy, would you put silverware and napkins around the table?"

"Yes, Mommy." She hopped down and went about her task as if she did this every morning.

"Lobsters is the way to go here in Maine," Mick was saying. "We get orders from all over the world. I'd say half the business comes from outside orders. Of course, summers it's the tourists. They're what keeps us going for sure."

"We were certainly busy last night."

"Do you like lobster?" Maddy asked, plunking a fork down on the napkin.

"I love them. And you?"

"They're okay, but I like peanut butter and jelly the best."

"You better not have her do any commercials for TV," Aaron said.

They all laughed and finished breakfast. It would be a busy day, and there were things to do.

four

Aaron felt a warm, pleasant feeling inside. Deanna's cooking was better than Cora's. He hadn't been this full since the buffet he'd found in Bangor. He could tell Deanna enjoyed cooking. Some women, like his mother—what little he could remember of her—cooked because they had to. It was an argument he remembered hearing from early childhood.

"Cooking is a chore I detest," his mother had said. He remembered the fiery look in her eyes as she pointed the spatula at his father. "I'd never cook another meal if I didn't have to."

Funny that he should think about that now. He followed Mick out the door and down the steps.

"We have lots to do around here." The older man wore an old parka with hood and patches on the elbows. He hunkered down in an effort to keep the cold wind out.

"My son handles the boat now. I used to help on the boat, but he has a local lad now, and they bring in what they can. Some days are better than others."

"I wondered about going out sometime. You know, set the bait or whatever."

"GB is licensed. Maine is particular about that. I have other jobs in mind for you, Son."

Aaron nodded. At home the oystermen and crabbers were also licensed. Why would it be different here?

"I'll be happy to do whatever you want. I did notice the building is in need of paint."

"We should have gotten that done earlier in the year, but if we get a good day between now and winter, we'll just do it."

Aaron nodded. "I can paint, clean up, and also wait on

customers—whatever you want."

A voice sounded, and Maddy came running down the hill, as well as she could run. Bundled in a snowsuit, fur cap, and mittens, she looked delightfully roly-poly; Aaron stifled a laugh.

"That daughter of mine—she's overprotective. If Maddy has the slightest little sniffle, out come the winter clothes, and she'll check her forehead every hour on the hour."

Aaron sensed the older man loved his daughter and the grandchild more than he wanted to let on.

"She's all she has," Aaron offered then.

Mick leaned against the railing close to the pound box. "That's so. You know about that, do you now?"

Aaron nodded. "Yes. I guessed that there's no father around."

"He shouldn't have gone out in the boat that day. Crazy fool! He wanted Maddy and Deanna to go along, but Deanna wisely said no, that she'd heard a storm was brewing and she'd rather stay home with Maddy."

Maddy finally reached them and hugged her grandfather's leg. "Grandpa, Mommy says I can stay with her in the office until you go up to watch the news."

"That so?" He pulled the pipe out of his pocket and stuck it between his teeth. He did not light it, and Aaron wondered if he ever did.

"Grandpa, Mommy also said you should turn the heater on in the office."

"That's exactly what I had in mind." He reached down and grabbed her. She giggled and pretended she wanted to escape.

Aaron leaned over and tickled her under the chin. He remembered how Hannah had liked that at this age.

She smiled back and grabbed his hand.

"Are you two going to stand out here all morning and lollygag?" The voice was sharp, but the eyes held merriment.

"Oh. You here already?"

"Well, Dad, someone has to work. The books are done on

the fifteenth of the month and this is the fourteenth."

Deanna unlocked the door and turned on the light. "Brrr, it's cold, and it isn't even close to winter yet."

Maddy ran inside and turned the heater on. All it took was the push of a button.

"Mommy, can we go to the store today? I'm all out of Cap'n Crunch."

"There's oatmeal, Madison."

"Can I have raisins in it?"

"Of course."

Aaron glanced up and found Deanna's gaze unwavering. He smiled and felt that tug in his heart again. *Calm down, calm down,* he reminded himself. *This isn't to go any further.*

"Here are the jackets, hats, and boots that I mentioned earlier," Deanna said, opening a large oak door. "Help yourself."

"I'll buy a coat soon," he offered.

"No need." Mick stood in the doorway. "We got plenty of stuff others have left, so you might as well save your money."

Aaron picked out a heavy, navy blue pea coat; something about the navy blue with the emblems on the buttons appealed to him. Wool was always warm, and it held up well in stormy, wet weather. Of course, it would be warm in a few hours.

"I thought these work shoes would be okay. I wore them at the logging camp."

"Yes, they're fine."

"We really need the upper deck cleaned and disinfected," Deanna said. "It didn't get done the night before, and if we don't do it every day, it starts smelling pretty fishy."

"And the garbage also needs to be emptied," Mick added. "I think that should keep you busy for a couple hours."

"And maybe Aaron can pick up a few items at the store," Deanna suggested, looking at Maddy, who had found her box of crayons and a much-used coloring book.

"I wanna go to the store," she said, looking up with a green crayon in her mouth.

"Madison, get that crayon out of your mouth now."

The little girl dropped it and stuck out her lower lip. It was clear she was a mite spoiled and used to getting her own way.

"Well, I do wanna go to the store," she repeated.

"We'll see."

It was clear that the matter had been dismissed, at least for a little while.

Deanna looked at Aaron again and then pointed. "The cleaning supplies are in a closet upstairs." He could see that she was not one to waste time.

He went up, glancing back once because he sensed that eyes were on him. Deanna looked away abruptly, but Maddy waved a crayon at him.

The floors were messy. People obviously cracked their lobster with gusto, scattering shells everywhere. There were garbage cans for shells and another for soft drink cans, but still the table was smeared with melted butter, bits of lobster shell, and wadded-up napkins.

He would need hot water, plenty of soap, and a disinfectant, but first he'd clean off the tables and sweep up the mess.

This job reminded him of Oysterville. Who would have thought he would trade cleaning up in the cannery, where he cracked open oysters, for taking care of a lobster pound? Here he was more than three thousand miles away and doing the same type of work. He should have stayed at the logging camp. But then he would not have met Deanna.

It took an hour to empty the small garbage cans into the larger one and sweep the floor. Then, on hands and knees, he scrubbed with a stiff brush. The floor looked great when he finished.

"I don't think anyone has cleaned the floor like that since my wife died." Mick had climbed the stairs. Aaron hadn't heard him because the radio was playing downstairs.

"Did I do it right?"

"You sure did." The older man grinned. "The only problem is you have to do this every day."

"I know, Sir."

"Mick. I don't go for the 'sir' stuff."

"Okay."

Aaron leaned back and poured a cup of coffee from the thermos Mick had handed him. The two sat at a clean table and looked out over the water.

"You know, I'm going to have to sell the Pound one of these days."

"You are?" For some reason Aaron could not imagine it being sold, just as he couldn't imagine his father ever selling the cannery in Oysterville. "But why?"

"GB doesn't want it. He has some notion about going to Massachusetts and doing something else. Deanna will go and get married on me and be raising more kids in some little white house with red trim, and I'm way too old to worry about it anymore."

"It should be kept in the family," Aaron said. "I don't think Deanna is going to leave."

"She can't operate the boat, bait the traps, and all that—"

"With help she could." Aaron set down his empty mug. "Have you asked her about it?"

"Don't have to. Women don't do those things."

"And why not?"

"She's got the kid, and that takes up a lot of her time. Now if I'd had more sons, or my wife had lived. . ." Pain momentarily etched his face. "Not that I'm not thankful for what the good Lord gave me."

Aaron picked up the bucket of dirty water and then set it down again. "I'd talk to her about it if I were you. Make sure what it is that she wants."

"To get married again. I know it. She's told me before."

"Maybe she's not ready for that."

The old man's eyes narrowed as he looked at Aaron. "How would you be knowing that when you just arrived here yesterday?"

"Because I think she still loves her husband. It's that simple."

Aaron thought of his father and how long it had been before he got his wife out of his mind. Aaron wondered if he had ever, in fact, succeeded. He never dated, never seemed to want to.

"I'll talk to her, but I'm in no rush about this. We have a good season coming up, and we ship our lobsters all over the world, you know. Thanksgiving and Christmas are busy times. Most people think about turkeys and hams, but we have our regular customers who order for the holidays."

"Dad! Aaron! Are you ready for lunch? I'm going up to the house to throw some food together."

"Yeah, sounds good," Mick answered. Then to Aaron he said, "Now, can you imagine that? How on earth do you throw food together?"

"With great care."

"Of course, it will be good. It always is."

Aaron laughed. "Well, I see I'm going to put on weight if I stay here very long."

The old man turned on the top step and almost glowered. "You are going to stay, young man, aren't you?"

"I said I'd stay a month, at least."

"A month! I'm going to need you longer than that."

Aaron grabbed the pea coat he'd left on the bench, having worked up a sweat while performing his job. "I won't leave you dangling," he said.

And as he walked down the steps, he knew he couldn't wait to be in the sunny, warm kitchen watching Deanna as she stood at the stove, then came to the table and said grace before they ate whatever it was that she had fixed. He might stay a long time, a really long, long time after all. . . .

৵

It was after lunch and the dishes had been done when Deanna suggested they go on into town and get supplies. "We can drop the garbage off on the way."

"And pick up Cap'n Crunch?" Maddy asked.

Deanna laughed, and he liked the way her mouth turned up. He found himself wanting to touch her, wanting to grasp one of the curls, wanting to feel how soft she would be in his arms. He shook his head and reached for his lightweight jacket.

The afternoon was warmer, and he slid into the front seat of the car next to Deanna. She drove an old, dented Chevy, the car she'd learned to drive in, she explained to him as she backed around and drove up out of the driveway.

"I like to drive," she said then. "And you?"

"Yes, when I have dependable wheels."

"One can always take a bus—"

"I like to ride a bus," Maddy interjected in her chirpy voice.

"Yes, Honey, I know you do."

"I get to ride the bus to Sunday school."

"You do?"

"The church we attend has a bus that picks up kids, and it works quite well."

"I'd like to go to church while I'm here."

"I think you'd like our church. It's small and friendly. I know most of the people, as we don't move around much in Maine, not like people out West."

"How do you know about people out West?" He felt he had to know.

"Well, look at you. I think you're from the West, even though you don't say. You just sound like it."

"Is that a fact?"

She glanced over and smiled one of those special, warm smiles that touched his heart. Again. "Yes, it is."

"Is that bad?"

She tilted her head as she pulled into the recycling center. "No, not at all."

"Mommy, why are you looking at Aaron like that?"

Her face turned a bright red, almost as red as the lobsters in the boiling vat.

"Because she likes me." There, he'd said it, but the words surprised even him.

"Everyone likes Aaron," Deanna said then. "I just know that about you."

Aaron wished, oh, how he wished. . . He would like nothing better than to go to his father and be welcomed with a hearty hug and a clap on the back, but Leighton hadn't even tried to find him. If he'd tried, Aaron could have been found. There were private investigators who did that sort of thing.

"Some day you must tell me about your family," Deanna said as she unbuckled Maddy from her car seat.

"Some day I might, but it's a pretty boring story."

"I bet it won't be to me."

A couple of heads turned as they entered the store, and Aaron smiled. It was a small town where everybody knew everyone. It was like that at home too.

One young woman was particularly bold as she stepped up. "Hi, Deanna. Who's your friend?"

Deanna introduced him as Aaron, who now worked for the Lobster Pound. Aaron nodded, and they moved on.

"Dottie has always been nosy," was Deanna's explanation. "Don't pay any attention to her."

Maddy wanted in the shopping cart, even though she was big, so Aaron lifted her up and set her on the seat.

"It's better this way," Deanna said then. "Now she can't grab food on the shelves."

"Tell me what kind of meat you like," she said after picking up the cereal, a gallon of milk, and two loaves of bread.

"I haven't been able to choose in so long, I don't know

what to say. I like everything. I really do."

She selected a roast, large package of pork chops, a turkey breast, and some ground beef. "I'm sure you'll get tired of lobster."

"Does your brother ever come over later?" Aaron asked.

"GB isn't much to mingle. He goes out way before light and comes back in, brings in the pots, and leaves. Seeing the catch of the day is something Dad still enjoys."

"Can you imagine ever doing anything else?" Aaron asked. If the old man wasn't going to ask, he would.

"Why, what do you mean?" She reached over and took a box of candy away from Maddy; she'd just been able to reach it by stretching her little arms out.

"Have you ever thought of living somewhere else, away from the Pound?"

Her eyes looked startled. "Why, no. Why would I?"

It was as Aaron figured. This was her home, her life. She had no intention of moving on, not even if a man came along and swept her off her feet. . . . Deanna turned and eyed him with a puzzled look. "Why do you ask?"

He wanted to tell her about the earlier conversation with her father but didn't feel it was right to do so. "Just wondering is all."

Maddy started reaching for a package of gum this time, and Deanna turned her around and made her sit up straight. Aaron was glad for the diversion. Why had he asked her anyway?

She paid for the groceries while Aaron stuck a quarter in a coin-operated mechanical horse and, after asking Deanna's permission, put Maddy on its back.

Her curls bounced as the little girl laughed with glee. She was an easy child to love. Her mother was even easier. And with a sudden fear, Aaron knew he was not going to like moving on. He was not going to like it at all.

five

That second night, Aaron thought about his good fortune. He had a roof over his head, a job, and there was a woman with eyes that twinkled and a gaze he couldn't put out of his mind. It was the myriad of thoughts that tripped him up.

He thought of Jill back in Oysterville. They'd dated his junior year. She was cute too, with eyes that captivated him, but that was a long time ago. Jill probably was married and had a baby by now.

As always when he thought of home, his mind went to Hannah. He had prayed, telling her that it would get better. It has to, he always said to himself. Things can't get much worse. He had prayed for a miracle, but it didn't happen. And because of it he had run as far as he could go. He had not attended church in months, and God seemed very far away.

Aaron listened to the sounds of waves lapping against the shore, down the hill from the cottage. The smell, the feel of the place, reminded him of Oysterville—yet it was different. The bay here was calmer, though he supposed that when a storm blew up, the waves would toss and the wind would howl around the house. He remembered looking out his basement bedroom window at home, watching the aspens sway back and forth, their branches interlocked, the leaves in a frenzied state as they fluttered in the wind. Fir trees withstood the wind better, dropping a needle or two, as Willapa Bay was stirred to frothy waves of gray and blue. Sometimes he'd grab his long jacket and a stocking cap and run out the door, then tear off down the path to watch from the water's edge. In the earlier days, he'd taken Hannah with him. He didn't think his father ever knew about their night adventures.

Later, when Hannah grew more frail, he'd hear her coughing and knew she'd been awakened by a storm. Sometimes he went to her room and held her hand. Words weren't needed as they listened to the storm, wondering if the wind would die down by daylight. Usually it did.

Aaron felt his heart nearly squeeze shut. He should never have left her. How many times had he gone over the scene in his mind, knowing, wishing he'd been there for her. Why did people fear being around dying people when family and friends were what they needed the most? Would the guilt ever stop?

ð

Aaron opened the door to the cottage and slipped outside. He didn't have shoes but wore heavy wool socks and an old pair of slippers. He wouldn't go far, but he wanted to see where the path went that ran along the front of the cottage. The night was lit by a full moon, its rays shining on the water below. He breathed deeply of the night air, noticing the pungent smell of pine. Maine was called the Pine Tree State for good reason. The air smelled different from that in Oysterville.

He wore his jeans, grimy from a day of cleaning the mess on the upper floor. He wore nothing over the T-shirt. The night was cool, but he shivered once and then became accustomed to it. He'd become used to the cold winters in northwestern Maine. He breathed deeply again. Hearing a twig crack, he thought it was probably an animal on the path ahead. A light beamed up and down along the path, several yards to the north. Aaron ducked behind a tree, not wanting to be seen. The sounds came closer, the light illuminating the tree branches and shrubbery that grew along the narrow path.

And then he saw it was Deanna. She was dressed in a long coat, her hair bouncing as she hurried along the trail. The flashlight swung back and forth. She came closer, and he knew she might pick up his shadow or even his scent. Then he heard Murphy. The dog would give him away for sure, so Aaron stepped out.

Deanna stopped and gasped. He could barely make out her outline and couldn't see her eyes but sensed her fear.

"It's just me," he said. "I couldn't sleep, and it was such a beautiful night."

"Oh, my goodness, you scared five year's growth from me!"

Murphy bounded around the bend and wagged his tail when he saw Aaron.

"Do you often go alone on a midnight stroll?" he asked.

She set down the flashlight. "Oh, no. Rarely. At least not this time of year. Besides, as you can see, I'm not alone. Of course, Murph stops to sniff every bush he sees." She hugged the black Lab close.

Murphy nudged Aaron's hand. "Yes, I'm okay now. You've decided I can stay, is that it, Fella?" He ruffled the dog's thick fur, and Murphy came back for more.

"Murph's not a good watchdog, but he'd protect me if anyone tried to hurt me." She hesitated for a moment, as if she couldn't think of what to say next. The silence was awkward as Aaron took a deep breath.

"I like late-night walks. Always have." *We must be alike in that way,* he couldn't help thinking.

"So do I." She nodded as she passed in front of him, then turned and looked back. "But morning will be here before we know it. Do stop in for breakfast. It makes Dad happy to have someone to talk to."

And what about you? Aaron wanted to ask, but the words stayed deep inside him.

He waited until she disappeared. Once, Murphy looked back, as if expecting Aaron to follow.

If he thought he couldn't sleep before, he definitely couldn't sleep now. Not with visions of bouncing curls and deep, deep brown eyes dancing through his mind.

❦

Aaron thought again about the night he'd left home, carrying the duffel. He had no idea where he was headed. He just had to get away, and later he'd think about returning.

He'd climbed in back of a pickup that had stopped at a tavern, covering himself with a tarp. Probably the driver wasn't going far, but he'd ride for a few miles. Surprisingly, the truck headed south, then off the peninsula; soon it was driving over the Astoria-Megler Bridge. He was getting as far as Oregon at least. Maybe he'd take a bus. He had some money stowed in a sock at the bottom of the backpack. His shoes were almost new, and his jacket was sturdy and in good condition. He had one change of clothes and two chunks of Cora's cornbread left over from dinner the night before.

The truck finally came to rest in the driveway of an older home located in a neighborhood of what Aaron guessed was Portland or one of the city's suburbs. He waited for a few minutes, then threw off the tarp, climbed out of the truck bed, and headed off toward the glow of lights in the sky that he knew emanated from the heart of the city. He would ask for directions to the bus station as soon as he reached a business that was open all night.

The bus took him to Idaho. There were no questions asked. Nobody said, "Hey kid, aren't you kind of young to be traveling alone?"

Aaron was so hungry by the time the bus arrived in Boise, he could have eaten a possum. His money wouldn't go far, so he'd need to look for work soon. He finally decided Boise was as good a place as any. And that's how he managed. He worked a few weeks here, a few there, then traveled north to Montana. He'd considered going south but had heard they were hiring cowboys in Montana, and he'd always thought about living on a ranch someday. It would be different from living with water surrounding you on three sides. He'd seen lots of mountains, tall trees, and a few lakes, but nothing that compared to the Columbia River, the Pacific Ocean, and Willapa Bay on the peninsula.

It turned out there were no jobs in Montana, so he stayed in North Dakota for awhile, later moving on to Minnesota and then Wisconsin; and it was there that he stayed the longest, working on a dairy farm. He liked the owner, and the house was nice, with a bedroom all his own. He bought an old pickup with two hundred thousand miles on it, and one morning after thinking about Hannah, he knew he had to keep moving.

Not once had he written or called home, and the more time that passed, the more he knew he could not do it. His father would light into him for being disrespectful, and what was the idea, his running off and not even finishing high school? "What's gotten into you, anyway?" was the usual question thrown at him at every turn. His father, once a gentle giant, by this time seemed angry about everything and at everybody. Aaron couldn't help it that Hannah was sick. Didn't his father know Aaron loved Hannah just as much as his father did?

After the pickup, Aaron bought Levi's, wool shirts, underwear—all the things a young man needs for wintertime—and stashed them in a footlocker he'd found at a yard sale. He left Wisconsin, driving instead of hitchhiking or hopping freight.

Weeks before, he had mailed a money order to his hometown to subscribe to the local paper, the Chinook Observer, asking that it be sent to him general delivery at the small Wisconsin town. Later, he'd sent a change of address request when he settled for a few weeks. He had to keep track of things back home, though he had no intention of returning. At one time he had considered doing so, but now he knew he wasn't going to go home. Not yet. Maybe never.

In Michigan, Aaron worked in a car lot selling used cars,

but he was miserable. He didn't have the ability to sell any-thing. The only good that came of it was that he traded the pickup for a car with fewer miles. A month later he drove into northern Ohio, up through Cleveland, and on to Erie, Pennsylvania. From there he traveled along the southern tier of New York. There he worked at an artist's studio.

Tammy had needed someone to do screen painting on T-shirts, and he liked the work. It was a beautiful little town on the shore of Lake Champagne, and he realized once again how much he'd missed the waters of home. He rented a cabin and decided to stay for the winter. And winter he did have, with blowing snow that almost buried the cabin. But even though he was cold, with the cabin never warmer than sixty degrees, he looked out at the lake with great fondness. He just might not leave here. Besides, Tammy brought him dinner almost every night, and she was an excellent cook.

Tammy had told him her daughter was away at college, but would be home for the holidays. Once again Aaron was included in a family's home. It didn't make him long for home, because he could not remember ever having a home with a mother and a father. His mother had taken off when he was four, and though Cora looked after the house, it wasn't the same at all. He suspected that Cora would have liked to marry his father, but Leighton dated no one and did not ever plan to marry again. He had told Aaron this one afternoon while they picked oysters and packed them in boxes for shipping.

"But maybe I would like a mother. Tom would; he told me so."

Leighton had shaken his head. "Sorry to disappoint you, Son, but I have no desire to travel that path again."

"Do you believe in God?" Aaron wondered later why he had asked the question, but he'd felt he had to know.

"Of course I do." He had leaned over and ruffled Aaron's hair. "I can see I've been neglecting you. What do you say we drive into Portland tomorrow? I need to pick up some supplies, and we can eat at that café down at the square and maybe go watch the boats come up the Willamette. How about it?"

It was one of the last good times they'd had, and one of the few Aaron could even recall. Christmas and other holidays were observed, but there was no joy in the celebration. His brothers seemed to draw toward each other, but all Aaron had was Hannah, and she was dying.

"Hello?" A voice had broken through his thoughts as he'd sat looking out over the lake. Aaron glanced up to see a dark-haired young woman standing at the end of the pier.

"You must be Shellie, Tammy's daughter."

"Yes, I am." She laughed, and he froze up, thinking how she sounded just like Hannah.

"I'm going to have a cup of tea. Would you like some?"

They'd been inseparable for two weeks; he'd even convinced her that a good coffee was better than tea any day. Then she left to return to college, though she said she'd write and be home again in two months. Aaron felt his heart soar and looked forward to seeing Shellie again. But after a week of feeling bereft, he decided he couldn't stay, that he would never let his heart love again. It hurt too much.

He left the next morning before Tammy and her husband awakened. He wrote a note and pinned it to the door, thanking them for their kindnesses and saying he hoped their business would continue to flourish.

Aaron traveled east, along the lower part of New York and then cut up through Poughkeepsie. He found a job in a newspaper office delivering papers; that lasted a month. He went up to Vermont and stayed a month, then crossed New Hampshire and headed into the northwest corner of Maine. He had done it. He had wanted to travel clear across the United States, and he had succeeded. His first job was in a toothpick factory, and there he stayed for a year. Then he got the logging job. It was good, and he enjoyed the outdoors work, hauling the boards by sled during the winter months, shipping them down the river once the ice floes broke up.

There were no more women that attracted him, but that was because he never smiled twice at anyone. Aaron moved on because a jealous coworker thought Aaron liked his wife. He didn't need that kind of trouble.

He wasn't sure how he ended up clear over on the eastern side of the state, but here he was, and it was the Lobster Pound that had caught his eye, prompting him to stop. Was it just two days ago when he arrived, found he liked it here, and wanted to stay?

And would he ever learn that women were to look at, talk to, but not to care too deeply about? It only caused heartache. His father had been right—who needed marriage? For that matter, who needed God? Hadn't Aaron done pretty well on his own these past years?

Aaron slipped out of bed and turned on the small bedroom light. He stared at the wedding gown again. A huge trunk was at the foot of the bed, but he didn't look inside. It was a good thing he didn't need more room, as this was the only closet. He'd been living out of his duffel for so long, he wouldn't know what to do with hung-up clothes.

Aaron guessed he'd just have to ask Deanna about the dress. It was too bad he wasn't looking for a wife, for he knew she'd be a good one. He thought of the little girl with the dimples and flyaway dark hair. He wanted to hold her close, as there was something about Maddy that reminded him of Hannah when she was younger.

Aaron pulled the sliding door shut. Deanna and her husband had lived in this cottage. They had come here after their wedding and had conceived a baby in the very bed he slept in. But the sea had taken him away. Well, it wasn't Aaron's responsibility to take away the look of loneliness he saw in her dark eyes when she thought he wasn't looking.

Finally he gave up the idea of sleeping and put some water on the stove, thankful he'd bought coffee the day before. There was nothing like a fresh cup of coffee at three A.M. Coffee was definitely an essential of life.

He looked at his reflection in the depths of his cup. Deanna came to mind again, and he tried to shake the thought. Maybe he'd better not stay here at all. It might not be a good idea, considering the way he was feeling. Not a good idea at all. . . .

six

Deanna hurried up the stairs and slipped into the house as quietly as possible. Her heart still pounded from seeing Aaron on the path moments ago, and she tried to ignore the way her mind raced. She hugged Murph impulsively and then went to the cupboard for his doggie treat.

She sat in the darkness again, though the hour was late and morning would come too soon. There was something about Aaron that puzzled her, and she wasn't sure what. His smile captivated her and made her feel alive again, like when she first loved Bobby. Now Maddy was the light of her life, and daily she thanked God for her precious child. She remembered hoping for a son to carry on Bobby's name, but Madison was the very likeness of her father, and perhaps one day she'd carry on his name with a hyphen for her new married name. But that was a long way off. . . .

The wind picked up, whistling around the house, a reminder of the changeable weather even in early September. Deanna reached for the afghan and slipped it over her shoulders. She had to go to bed; she would have to tell her mind to stop thinking. She wasn't ready for a relationship. It wouldn't matter how nice the person was. And the haunting look in Aaron's eyes told her he wasn't ready for one either. They would just be friends. It was better that way.

Leaving her boots at the door, Deanna headed up the stairs. Her father's heavy snores filled the whole upstairs of the house. She'd gotten used to it but remembered that when her mother was still living, her mother wore earplugs to bed.

Maddy was curled into a ball, her thumb in her mouth.

44

Deanna had given up trying to break her of the habit months ago. She didn't want her child sneaking around a corner to suck her thumb. And she'd thrown the pacifier away when Maddy wasn't even a year old.

She pulled the covers up under Maddy's chin and bent down to kiss her forehead. A swell rose in her chest as she looked at her child. Such a blessing. What a miracle a child was. How could anyone ever abuse children? It was beyond her comprehension. She got on her knees and said her evening prayers, asking for guidance, for safety, and for health for all. "And, Lord, if it isn't asking too much, I ask for GB to catch lots of lobsters tomorrow and on into winter."

Maddy rolled over, almost smacking her mother in the mouth with an outstretched arm, breathing that funny little catching sound. Deanna touched her soft hair once more, then tiptoed down the hall to her room. Maddy's room was the small one up under the eaves, a perfect room for a baby. Later, when she had more toys and dolls, she could have the larger room at the opposite end. They'd left the cottage after Maddy was born and came to the big house. Mick had insisted on it.

Deanna crawled into bed, but her mind wouldn't let her sleep. Her thoughts went back to when she'd first met her husband. He wasn't from Maine and had moved in with a brother. He came to church one Sunday, and later, they sat across from each other at the monthly potluck. He had been bold, almost brazen, from that first meeting. After they had their choice of pie, he asked if he could walk her home.

"If you want to walk two miles," she'd said.

"I don't have a car," was his answer.

"Oh." She assumed everyone his age had a car. "We could walk then. That would be okay."

And so they did. Shortly after that day, Bobby bought an old junker. Once he had wheels, he came calling almost every night.

It had been a whirlwind courtship, and when he asked her

to marry him two months later, she found herself saying yes.

"You hardly know the man," her father had argued.

"You're right, Dad," she retorted, "but I love him, and he loves me, and that's all I need to know."

He sighed, looking up from the lobster trap he was repairing. "Your mother would have wanted you to have a wedding."

"Dad, I don't need a big, fancy wedding. Really, I don't care about it."

"Your mother would come back to haunt me if I didn't give you away in the proper fashion."

In the end Deanna had relented, and everyone in Belfast was invited to the wedding of the year. Could she help it if most of the townspeople—who had known her mother since Deanna was young—wanted a chance to see Deanna married in the church with a white dress and all the trimmings?

She had found the dress in Bangor but took it back when her father scratched his head after looking at the price tag. "Four hundred for a dress?"

"Daddy, I told you I didn't need a big wedding."

"But this is ridiculous."

"There isn't time to have one made." Geneva was the town seamstress, and Deanna had thought of her, but she knew it took time to design, cut out, and put together something as fancy as a wedding dress. Then there were all the fittings. But her father insisted she ask, and Geneva set everything else aside and had the dress made to fit Deanna's small frame perfectly; she did it in a week's time.

The scalloped neckline and tiny pearl buttons at the waist were what Deanna ordered. There was just a small train, no sweeping one, and the veil was simple and one that Geneva had on hand for another young girl who had changed her mind about marriage the day before her wedding.

The gown was still in the cottage. That was why she couldn't believe her father would offer to let Aaron stay there. She kept saying she'd bring the dress up to the house, maybe get a few other items, such as wedding presents—some she had never used—as well, but that time had not come. And now a stranger was living there.

She wondered if Aaron had noticed the dress. Yet how could he not? Surely he would be hanging up clothes, and the dress would be quite noticeable, even if it were pushed to the back of the closet.

Deanna closed her eyes, and it was Aaron's eyes, Aaron's smile, that floated through her mind, not Bobby's. Was she to the point of forgetting her husband, Maddy's father? Was it time to think of a father for Maddy? A permanent father? Her grandpa paid her a lot of attention, and when GB came around, Maddy clung to him like a lost lamb. Yes, she supposed Maddy needed a father in her life, yet Deanna had to be sure it was someone who loved Maddy as if she were his own, and how many men could do that?

There was a secret in Aaron's blue eyes. Had he left a loved one behind? And did he even have a home? If so, where? Maybe he was an orphan. He hadn't said, just stated that he was looking for a job and would do just about anything for whatever pay they could give him.

Deanna closed her eyes again and thought about her walk along the water's edge. She had walked every night after Bobby died, even in the winter. She'd lost weight and was just starting to fill out her clothes again. Now she was feeling like walking, and apparently Aaron was also. Did people who stayed up at night have lots on their mind? Or if one went walking, did it indicate that there were things he or she was worried or concerned about?

Since she couldn't sleep, Deanna threw off the covers, turned on the small lamp across the room, and foraged through the top drawer for the photo album. Perhaps looking at Bobby would bring back a sense of contentment. It was worth a try.

❧

Aaron sat, sipping his second cup of coffee, realizing that if he were to get up and go to work, he needed some shuteye. Finishing his coffee, he set down the cup and lay on the bed, fully clothed.

Once he was asleep, the dream came again. Hannah was reaching out and crying for him to help her, to pound on her back, to make her better.

"Hannah, I cannot help," he said. "Nobody can. One day you're going to heaven to be with Jesus."

Aaron woke up, his shirt wet with sweat, realizing it was that same dream, the one he always had when his life was in turmoil. Why had he come here? Why didn't he leave in the morning, tell them he'd made a terrible mistake, that he really must be moving on. He'd say that he had a dying uncle in Massachusetts or make some such excuse. Crumb, he didn't need to give a reason. He hadn't even unpacked his duffel bag. He could send money later, to cover his lodging.

He had his jeans and his boots on when he realized he couldn't go. He didn't want to go. He would stay. Give it a month. He'd keep it casual. Nod hello, answer questions Deanna might have, talk to Maddy now and then, and of course, be friends with Murphy. One could not ignore a dog. They didn't allow it. They asked no questions, nor did they demand anything but love and attention. He could handle that. Yes, he could definitely do that. He'd stay. At least for now.

He undressed and crawled under the covers, where sleep came, and this time it was a peaceful, restful sleep. He slept until five A.M., when a ship's horn blasted from the bay, causing him to shoot out of bed, his feet slipping on the throw rug beside the bed.

seven

When morning came, Aaron wondered again what had led him to this particular lobster pound. There had been others farther north along the shoreline, and there would probably be more south, should he venture that way, which was his inclination. What had led him to go off the main road, driving down the winding road until he was in front of the huge white building with its inviting sign?

Had God led him here? He wasn't sure how he felt about God's leading. It seemed that some believed in God's provision and guidance far more than did he. And yet, he could never deny that it was God who had helped him through several situations over the past five years.

Deanna would be bustling around in the big house, but he didn't want to interrupt her time for devotions. She needed that to recoup. He wondered if she'd have scrambled eggs again, or would it be something different? It was Sunday morning, and he knew the family attended church. Should he go with them if he was invited?

He pulled back the curtain and looked out the window. Morning light was seeping through the clouds, but a layer of fog clung to the shoreline like hair on a dog's back. Typical weather for here, just as it had been back home. Many mornings, Aaron had walked to catch the school bus in the fog. Winters had been rainy, and he wondered if it also rained a lot here on the eastern seaboard. He hadn't seen much inland. Someone had told him it was warmer along the shore. Last winter it had snowed. It snowed and snowed and snowed some more, until he got sick of the stuff. That had been the winter of

logging, a job he'd never thought he would like. And yet he
had liked the logging camp and the men he worked with. Now
he knew what it meant to log the woods—how one had to bundle up or freeze. At home you bundled up to keep dry; here it
was to keep warm. He'd never been so cold!

A figure came up from the dock. GB. He'd stayed home yesterday and came early today to check the traps. Minutes later a
horn sounded, and Aaron knew he had left for the day's work.

Aaron finished the last of his crackers and had a second cup
of coffee. Even if Deanna had prepared a big breakfast, he'd
still be hungry. Funny how it worked; you could make do with
a few stale crackers, but let someone set a plate of ham and
eggs in front of you, and you could wolf it all down in minutes.

He laced his boots, checked the stove, threw the cover up
over the bed so it looked made, then opened the door.

It was only five. Hadn't Deanna said to come at six? That
meant he had awhile to walk to the docks, wishing more than
anything that he owned a boat, that he could go out and
empty the pots, add more bait, and bring home the day's
catch. Maybe he'd get to do that yet.

Aaron looked at the holding tank, watching the lobsters
swim. They were actually ugly, and it wasn't until they were
boiled that they became the beautiful red color. The counter
where people ordered was ready for business, and the office
was beyond that. Through the window he could see the sign
up over the desk. It read:

> *The pessimist complains about the wind,*
> *The optimist expects it to change,*
> *The realist adjusts the sails.*
>
> WILLIAM ARTHUR WARD

Aaron liked the saying. It was so true and totally appropriate for
here on the coast. He felt he was a cross between an optimist

and a realist. He wondered what Deanna was. Definitely not a pessimist. Perhaps GB was, though. He came across that way to Aaron.

He walked around the side of the building. It needed new paint. He had noticed that yesterday, but in the morning light it was more evident. Chipped paint on the east side due to the harsh winds—he'd heard this meant one had to paint just about every year. It was then he saw Deanna in the window of the big house. She was looking out, and he waved heartily. She waved back, and his heart did that funny little lurch it had done last night when he'd seen her coming down the path.

He took a deep breath, deciding to head up to the house after all. Maybe he could get a better perspective on what was expected of him today. Mick had not said much last night, just that he had plenty to do before the Pound opened for business.

"I need another pair of hands, Son. These are old and arthritic." He held them up for Aaron to see. They were bent and gnarled, the nails thick and yellowed. He could see that those hands couldn't do much work. So, he would be the hands and the legs too for Mick. Yes, he could do that. Now if he could just keep Deanna in the right place in his mind. . .

ঌ

Deanna had seen him walk down to the Pound. Hands in his pockets, hunched over, he seemed to be inspecting the side of the building. Maybe he could do the needed repairs, spruce the place up a bit, maybe even paint it—all jobs Bobby would have done had he lived.

At the thought of her husband, the lump returned to her throat. It was over, and no amount of wishing would bring him back. "You must get on with your life," Pastor Neal had said. "Life is for the living, Deanna. Perhaps there is someone out there who needs a wife and a child. I know God will provide. Just be strong in your faith."

She smiled, thinking of the verse she'd come across this morning. It spoke to her heart, and she had written it in her journal:

> *"Thou hast turned for me my mourning into dancing: thou hast put off my sackcloth, and girded me with gladness;*
> *To the end that my glory may sing praise to thee, and not be silent. O Lord my God, I will give thanks unto thee for ever."*   PSALM 30:11–12

It was Sunday, and Deanna looked forward to attending church. Maddy liked Sunday school, and she needed the interaction with other children her age. If Deanna had more time, she might have looked into a preschool for Maddy, but in reality, she felt safer keeping her at home with her. At least for now.

Would Aaron attend church with them? He'd mentioned doing so when they went to the store, so she would ask. He couldn't do any more than say no, and he just might say yes.

She walked away from the window, remembering how the young man had looked down on the dock, hands thrust in his pockets. It was time to get busy with breakfast preparations. She wondered if Aaron liked pancakes as well as her father and Maddy did. Maybe she'd make them special today. She had overripe bananas and nuts. This had been a favorite of her mother, and Deanna loved making them for the family.

She was beating egg whites into a heavy froth when the knock sounded, the door opening slightly.

"Do you suppose I could come in and get a cup of your good coffee?"

She smiled as she waved him in. "I've got the coffee ready and am starting pancakes now. I hope you like bananas and walnuts."

Aaron grinned. "Our housekeeper made banana-nut pancakes, and it's one of my fondest memories."

Deanna almost dropped the spoon. "Are you serious? You're not just saying that. . . ."

"No, I mean it."

"I've never known anyone else who made them."

Their glances met, and Aaron wondered what it would be like to have Deanna whipping up meals in his kitchen. He decided it would be nice and something he'd never tire of.

"Would you like to attend our church this morning?"

"What about work? I have the upper deck to clean up before customers arrive."

She laughed. "Have you not heard that thou shalt rest on the seventh day?"

"You mean you don't open on Sunday?"

"Well, no, we do open, but not until three, so there will be plenty of time."

Aaron said yes, he would like to go, then helped set the table, since neither Maddy nor Mick was up yet. It felt good to be working in the kitchen next to Deanna. He liked the feeling. He liked her. He definitely had some rethinking to do.

eight

That first week was a learning experience. Aaron was the "gofer" at the Pound. Not that he minded. It was all work that needed to be done. Mick did what he could to maintain the place and kept busy mending broken traps, but there were days when he was "stove up" as he called it, and Deanna had taken over. This left her frazzled, as she wanted to spend time with Madison and also cook more, one of her favorite pastimes. Aaron worked hard, and consequently he discovered that he ate more.

He whistled now as he worked, cleaning up the restaurant on the top floor. He even had the steps clean and polished. The windows were the next things he tackled. It was amazing how people flocked to the Pound for a good Friday night lobster dinner. He'd met a lot of the local townspeople, along with travelers who had heard this was the place to stop for lobster. But he learned after that first night that they also served a variety of seafood, and Deanna had recently added chowders and stews to the menu.

And all the while, Aaron found himself pulled more and more toward Maddy and her mother. The child followed him around as he worked, and though Deanna called out suggesting that she should come down to the office to color or read one of her books, Maddy would beg to stay upstairs with him. She didn't get in the way. He rather liked the distraction.

One evening Deanna suggested a drive over to Stockton Springs to pick blueberries the next day. "It's the end of the season, and blueberries are Dad's favorite berry. He can get by with us gone for the morning. Let's get up early and take off by six, so we'll have plenty of time for picking."

"Mommy, can I pick blueberries too?"

"Of course. I have a bucket the right size for you."

"Mick will be okay?"

Deanna nodded. "Sure. We'll get back in time for me to fix Dad a good meal, and then later I'll make blueberry pies and put some in the freezer."

Her eyes sparkled as she spoke, and it was all he could do to keep from pulling her into his arms and running his hand through the thick thatch of curls. He looked away, then back again after he felt more composed.

"What if someone comes to the Pound?"

She grinned impishly. "We can put a sign on the door: 'Gone fishin'.' "

Maddy came up, dragging a doll by one arm. "Did you say we were going to go fishing?"

Aaron and Deanna both laughed as Deanna held her small daughter close. "No, Honey. Not fishing. We're going to pick blueberries."

"And I get to go too?"

"Of course," Aaron said.

That evening Deanna served pot roast from the midday meal, which Mick called dinner, and apple pie.

"I wish this was blueberry," she said to her father. She turned to Aaron. "You know that Maine is noted for its blueberries?"

She was teasing him now. Aaron nodded. "I picked blueberries last year. They grew wild in the valley there. The loggers laughed at me, but I loved them. Back home we have blueberries, but they are a larger berry and cultivated on farms. We call the smaller version a huckleberry."

"Well, Daughter, my plate is empty, and you know what that means."

Deanna cut another slice of apple pie, topping it with a dollop of whipped cream. "My father loves his pie more than anything."

"Can't argue with that. Go on, Son. Have another piece. There's more when this one is gone, right?"

Deanna cut a second slice for Aaron as well, then gave Maddy a tiny sliver as of course she was clamoring for more too. "There's enough for GB to have a piece if he wants one after bringing the boat in."

"You going somewhere?" Mick looked up, his fork poised in the air.

"In the morning, Dad. I told you, remember? Aaron, Maddy, and I are taking a short trip over to Stockton Springs to pick blueberries."

"When are you getting back?"

"In plenty of time to open up."

"Oh. Well, it isn't as if you two haven't worked hard this week. And the weather won't hold, that's for sure."

❧

Aaron stayed up late drinking coffee that night. He thought of all the things he had not yet done, places he had not explored, and wondered if that was why he felt torn. Deanna kept coming to mind. He had nothing to offer and definitely felt marriage, which most women wanted, was not in the offing. Not now. Probably never.

The sky was dark with a low layer of clouds when Aaron stepped outside. Blueberry picking would be fun and a change of pace. He'd wear the only casual pants he owned. A bullet-gray knit sweater would lend warmth.

He walked up to the kitchen, expecting to see Deanna bustling around. She was not. He opened the door and went in. There was no fragrant smell of coffee brewing or rolls in the oven. Was something wrong? Had he misunderstood? He didn't want to call out in case she was still asleep.

He thought about the morning newspaper and went back out to fetch it from the box at the top of the hill. He could go back and heat up water for instant coffee too. He decided to go back to the big house.

Voices came from upstairs. One was Mick's, and he didn't sound happy. Should he go up to see if he could help? But what if Deanna was in her nightclothes? No, that would not do at all.

A voice called out. "Aaron? Are you there? I thought I heard the door close." She stood at the top of the steps, dressed in Levi's and a cherry-red sweater, her hair loose and free.

"Do you need something?"

"It's Dad. I can't leave him like this."

"Why? What's wrong?" He started up the steps.

"He had a bad night and won't go back to bed. Someone must be here to answer questions, should anyone come, and I don't want him down there working. It's just too hard for him."

Aaron was on the landing now, close enough that their shoulders touched as he started to move past.

"Well, I agree. He shouldn't be left. So what's the problem?"

"He says to go on; he wants us to have a good time."

"There are more days. . ."

Deanna smiled, stepped on her tiptoes, and impulsively kissed his cheek. "I knew that's what you'd say. I told Dad that. You're such a positive-thinking person, I knew you'd say we should just reschedule."

Maddy was in the hall and threw her arms around Aaron's legs. "I never thought you'd come upstairs," she cried, hugging him hard.

Aaron stepped back, as if realizing he was up in the confines of the old house. It was not right that he was here, and yet she had called out to him.

"I came to see your grandfather."

Mick's voice blustered from a room down the hall. "Drat and colored goat feathers! I can take care of myself! Been doing it ever since I was knee-high to a grasshopper!"

"Now, Dad. . ."

He was in the hall now, a robe thrown over long johns. "I insist that you leave me here. If I get worse, I'll call 9-1-1 or maybe someone from church. I say you need to go and pick those blueberries—have some fun. 'All work and no play makes Jack a dull boy,' as my mommy used to say."

Aaron stepped forward and put an arm around the old man's shoulder. "Mick, we can wait for our fun day. Really, it's okay. Placate Deanna. She would not have one ounce of fun if we left you behind feeling like this."

"Oh, you young whippersnappers! Think you got all the answers!"

"Grandpa!" Maddy tugged on his robe. "I think you'd better get dressed or go back to bed."

They laughed, and Deanna scooped her daughter into her arms. "You tell him, Honey."

"I want Aaron to carry me downstairs." Maddy turned to face him.

"Maddy, you must get dressed first. Then I'll come up and get you if you meet me halfway," Aaron said.

The upstairs had unconventional ceilings, with eaves on each side and small windows looking out at the bay on the west side, the road out another, and due east out the third. A flowered carpet covered the floor, and the doors were old and heavy with old-fashioned ceramic knobs. A dim light was in the middle of the hall, lighting the area as best it could.

"That's right. You've not seen the upstairs before," Deanna said. "It's really quite charming. Dad has the largest bedroom; it used to be his and Mother's, of course. Mine is the next largest, and Maddy has a tiny room at this end. No bathroom up here, which makes it quite unhandy, but I love the house—I especially love it upstairs here."

And I love you, popped into Aaron's mind before he knew it was there. How could he think such a thing? He smiled and started down the steep steps.

"I'm glad we're not going; it wouldn't be fun if you were worried about your dad."

"And I would worry. I'll be down as soon as I lay out Maddy's clothes."

Soon warmth filled the kitchen, and the smell of coffee made Aaron's stomach growl. He watched while Deanna put water on for her father's oatmeal—he never went without a bowl of oats in the morning. "That's what's kept me alive all these years," he claimed.

Biscuits were cut with a round cutter and placed on a baking sheet. Eggs were taken out of the refrigerator and set where they wouldn't roll off the counter. He was supposed to be reading the paper, but for some reason he couldn't get past the headlines, which was something about a crash of three vehicles near the state capitol.

"Dad is getting more cantankerous," Deanna said, turning around from the counter, an egg in each hand. "I have seen it coming for the past year or so. He wants his way. He forgets something, and then he seems to get mad at me when he forgets what I told him the day before."

"Aren't most older people that way?"

Aaron hadn't meant to be funny, but her eyes suddenly lit up in that way she had that made the thought come to mind again, *I love you, Deanna Barnes.*

"I've never been around many old people," she said, her face getting serious again. "Maybe a physical checkup would be the way to go, but he balks at that too. Doesn't want to see a doctor when he can still get out of bed and walk and eat. He is as stubborn as they come!"

"Let it go for now. Maybe we can come up with a plan. Let me think about it."

"You'd do that?"

"Sure. Why not?"

"But he isn't your family. . . ." Her words hung in the air, as if she realized too late what she'd said. He knew she had avoided talking about family in the past, and he was glad for it.

"He's my family now," Aaron said simply. *All the family I have,* he wanted to say.

Before she could answer, Maddy called from the stairs. "Okay, Aaron. I'm ready now! You can come get me and give me a piggyback ride."

"You spoil her," Deanna said as he pushed the paper aside and started up the stairs.

And she's my family too, he wanted to add.

☙

Deanna started beating eggs. Just as her father always had oatmeal, he also insisted that eggs should be part of the breakfast fare. Not that she minded. She didn't pay much attention to cholesterol, but perhaps it was time he did. No, it was time to seriously consider a full physical checkup for her father. It was long overdue. In fact, she couldn't remember the last time he'd even gone to a doctor. If he got a cold, which everyone did in the middle of winter, he took his favorite over-the-counter meds.

She watched while Maddy and Aaron came down the stairs, Maddy's shrieks filling the house. Maddy was so adorable, lovable, and needed a father. She looked at Aaron and the thought jumped to her mind: Could Maddy call Aaron "Daddy" some day? Would she like that? Deanna smiled as she whisked the eggs, then felt a hand touch her arm. She felt his presence, smelled his scent, without looking up.

"Yes?" she asked. But no more words came out as she felt his gaze meet hers, and she felt swept away with sudden longing. How could this be happening when she had loved Bobby so terribly much? How could she transfer those feelings to an absolute stranger she'd only known ten days?

"I said, can I help?"

"You can help me set the table," Maddy said, pushing past

her mother to the silverware drawer.

"I'll get the plates and bowls," Aaron said, reaching around Deanna.

For as large as the house was, the kitchen was fairly small—at least the workspace. They touched because he couldn't help it, and it was as if an electric spark went between them. He stepped back, the plates firmly in his hands.

"I think I'll go read the paper."

"Coffee's ready. Go sit, and I'll bring you a cup."

Mick entered the kitchen, leaning over, his hand over his left side as if he was having a problem walking. "It's the weather. Cold is coming. That's what my hip tells me."

"But there is medicine you can take, Dad. Dr. Anderson would prescribe it for you, but you must go in first."

"Humph!" He held his favorite mug out for Deanna to fill with coffee. "I am not taking any of those things. They tell you if you have high cholesterol, don't take it. If your heart's bad, don't take it. If you are constipated, don't take it. . . ."

"Dad!"

"Well, isn't it the truth? I am not going to take something that has all those side effects."

Deanna looked at Aaron and rolled her eyes. "Still, it's something we should check into."

Mick humphed again and grabbed a piece of the newspaper. Deanna knew that as far as he was concerned, the subject was closed.

Maddy chatted while she put all the chairs around the table just so. Then they sat, and Deanna glanced at Aaron over the top of her coffee mug. He smiled and then turned to Mick.

"Maybe I should paint the south side. What do you think?"

"Think the weather's going to hold?"

"I could paint one section and wait and see if it dries before tackling more."

They left the house. Sunshine filled him with hope. It always did. So far, East Belfast had not had much rain, nothing like the fall and winter rains in Oysterville. But the snow would come; even here in coastal Maine, snow came and stayed.

Murphy bounded over, wanting a scratch behind his ears and a pat.

"Hey, Boy, how are you this morning?" Already the young man and the dog had become fast friends. Murph wouldn't attack just anyone, but if someone started to harm his family, no telling what he might do, and Aaron knew the dog now considered him to be family. It was a good feeling.

After Maddy was bundled up, Deanna slipped on a coat and walked over to Aaron. "Thanks for being kind to my father."

"Kind?"

"Yes. . .you know." Her eyes met his and once again the feeling came over him. "He's so cantankerous, but you seem to know how to deal with him. I am at my wit's end at times, but he listens to you. I know he likes you."

And confides in me, Aaron wanted to say. Somehow, with her standing here, close enough for him to smell the faint scent of violets, he wondered if her heart hadn't mended and she just didn't know it yet.

"I think it will be a great day for painting, and I'll try to get this one wall done."

"Thanks again," Deanna said before turning and going inside the office. Maddy didn't want to go with her mother, but Deanna insisted, saying that she would get paint on her, and it was hard to get it off.

It would be white, of course, and maybe he'd suggest a trim. Red seemed appropriate. Red and white. He knew Deanna liked red. And suddenly he whistled a tune from *Fiddler on the Roof,* which took him back to a time when he and his father had been pals. Back when his father had loved him and thought him special. *Will I ever know a time like that again?* he couldn't help wondering.

nine

Aaron didn't get much chance to talk to GB, though he wished he could discuss the day's catch. GB came in and put the lobsters in the holding tank while Aaron was busy with customers. He'd see Maddy there, peering into the carrier.

"What a day!" he proclaimed one Friday; he stopped when he saw Aaron watching. Aaron didn't know what he'd done to make GB angry, but he wore a scowl when he looked in his direction. He'd seemed friendly when he'd talked about the Appalachian Trail that first day. Maybe he was upset because Aaron had spoken about going out in the boat. As if he would take over GB's position. He had no intention of doing such a thing.

"You can't go out on this boat!" GB had said that afternoon. His expression was harsh. "You need a license. Those are the rules."

Mick stopped hauling and looked from Aaron to his son. "He isn't taking your place. Not at all."

But from that afternoon on, GB tried to ignore Aaron, so Aaron stayed out of his way. No point in riling him up more. He was glad GB went home after the day's work. Things were unpleasant if he hung around, and he never wanted to cause friction between family members.

The lobsters were dumped into the holding tank. Three large, five medium-size, and one that measured right on the nose—just large enough. "Seen better days," GB said. "But this will add to the mix."

He scowled again at Aaron. "Thought you would be gone by now."

"GB!" Deanna looked at Aaron, as if wanting to see what his reaction would be. Aaron felt his face go hot but said nothing. It was often better to ignore people. If the old man needed an extra pair of hands, how could GB be against that? GB didn't help around the Pound, and Aaron worked at things Mick could no longer do. He wondered if GB knew how frail his father was.

"Don't listen to GB," Deanna said later, after GB had driven off in his pickup. "He thinks he's lord and master around here. Always has. He's such a crank at times!"

Aaron smiled. He understood only too well about brothers. At least Deanna only had to contend with one.

Aaron thought of GB a lot in the next few days. Mick seemed certain that GB wanted nothing to do with the business, yet his actions said otherwise. It appeared he cared very much what happened, and after Aaron had been in East Belfast two weeks with no signs of leaving, GB brought it up one afternoon over cups of coffee on the upper deck. Customers hadn't arrived, probably wouldn't for another hour.

"Dad, I mean no offense, but since things will be slowing down soon, don't you think the three of us can handle the Pound now?" He looked at Aaron. "Not anything against you, but my father doesn't have that much money."

Mick's chin jutted out. "Don't talk about me like I'm not here." He pointed his pipe at his son. "And how much money I have or do not have is my business. Besides, Deanna says more help means more customers."

"Deanna knows nothing about it! She's searching for something else." GB shoved his cup aside and stalked down the stairs. At the bottom he turned and shook his head. "I repeat, we can handle it!"

Deanna came out of the office, hands on hips. "Just go home, GB, and leave us alone!"

"Fine. Maybe I'll just quit, and you two can figure out who

is going to go out and bait the traps, dump 'em in, and go back later and haul 'em up! It isn't any party out there, Dee, and you, above all, should know that!"

Her cheeks went red, then white as she turned and ran up the hill to the house.

"That boy!" Mick said, pouring more coffee from the thermos. "He's like the lobster. He gets in the trap and then can't figure how to get out. He never has known when to just shut up. I think I know what's ailing him, but it's just too bad!"

"Maybe I should leave—"

"No, Son. I'm still making the decisions around here and will continue to do so until they put me six feet under."

Aaron knew what the drift was now. If he married Deanna, there would be less money for GB. Well, GB had nothing to worry about. Maybe he'd tell him the next time he saw him.

Deanna had gone off in a huff the same time GB left. Aaron guessed she was at the house. He decided to go on up and see if he could help, but halfway to the house, a car pulled into the Lobster Pound. He joined the people halfway down the hill.

"Evening."

The couple smiled and held hands as they went in to pick out lobsters, then ordered from the restaurant window where Mick stood. "I'll get these cooked for you in a minute."

"Do you want me to handle it, Mick?" Aaron offered.

"Guess you better, since Deanna is off at the house in a snit. Not that I blame her."

Aaron plunged the two lobsters into the boiling pot and timed it. The larger one had to stay in the water a minute longer. Mick got the butter ready, popped the French bread into the oven for a minute to heat, and got out the silverware.

"I could do this in my sleep," Mick said with a laugh. "But it's a good life; you know what I'm saying?"

Deanna and Maddy didn't come back to work, and Aaron

and Mick managed just fine. It was a light night. One never knew what to expect in the restaurant business.

Later that evening, when the Pound had closed down and the light meal was finished and Maddy had fallen asleep, Aaron got up from the sofa where he'd been reading Maddy's favorite book, *Blueberries for Sal*. He watched as Deanna carried the sleeping child up the stairs.

He sat on the couch and realized the house was quiet and that he enjoyed the silence. Soon the TV would go on, but for now, both Aaron and Mick seemed content to just sit.

"Don't hurt her, Son," Mick said, breaking the silence. "That's all I ask. Just don't hurt her."

Aaron was stunned. He said nothing for a long moment, choosing his words carefully.

"I would never hurt her intentionally."

Mick pulled his pipe out of his mouth. "I didn't reckon you would."

Aaron felt uncomfortable. He rose to his feet and nodded. "Busy day. Think I'll turn in early."

He had thinking to do. If he stayed here, he would never be good enough for Deanna, and if he weren't honest with her, Mick would have his neck. If he left without so much as a good-bye, he would forever see Deanna's dark, expressive eyes in his mind.

The night was nippy, a nippiness that one often felt on the bay during the winter. But it wasn't winter yet. Winter was three months off.

He got out the instant coffee, then decided to walk the path along the Bay. He had walked it on more than one occasion but had not run into Deanna again, though he had hoped to.

Was Deanna still in love with her husband? Would Bobby always hold a part of her heart? And if so, why could he think of nothing but taking her in his arms and proclaiming how he felt? Not that marriage was in the bargain. He knew most women wanted marriage, and that was the scary part.

The water was calm, and as a sliver of moon shone out of the darkened sky, it lit the path. Murph was suddenly there, and Aaron wondered how long he'd been trotting along behind him. And what was he doing here? He usually stayed at the house.

Then he heard her voice.

"Aaron!"

He stopped and waited for her to round the bend and catch up. "What are you doing out here?" He took her hand in both of his and held it tight. "You're freezing!"

"I know. I should have grabbed my gloves."

She wore a jacket with hood and boots. "I always forgot my gloves when I was little, and Mom would despair over me."

"When did your mother die?"

She looked past him, as if she couldn't quite meet his gaze. "I was in tenth grade. GB had just finished college."

"Your father told me it was cancer."

Deanna nodded. "Yeah. She'd had it a long time but never went to a doctor; nor did she tell any of us about the pain or the lump in her breast. . . ." Her voice broke.

Aaron's arm went around her as he pulled her to his chest. She clung to him as tears rolled down her cheeks. Murphy tried to wedge his way between the two and whined.

"He doesn't like to see me crying."

"Dogs are like that—there when you need a companion."

"Oh, Aaron, I do need a companion. I never realized it until the day you came. There was something about your eyes, your manner, and I hoped you'd stay on."

"You did?" Her hood fell back, and suddenly his mouth was against the curls; he held her as tightly as he dared.

"GB had no right to abuse you that way today. When I came back downstairs from putting Maddy to bed, I saw the empty chair where you always sit, and I thought you were leaving." She lifted her face. "I knew I couldn't let you go. I mean. . .I really like you. I know something else, Aaron."

"What's that?" He wanted time to stand still. He wanted to keep holding her, loving the way she felt in his arms, the feel of her head against his chest.

"I knew I never, ever wanted a day to go by when I didn't see your face," she finished.

Aaron was stunned for the second time that day. He cared deeply for Deanna, but her words meant more than caring. Her words talked of commitment, of being together in a permanent relationship. He couldn't do it. It might not work, just as his parents' relationship had not. Yet, he wanted to keep holding her as he listened to the lapping waves of the Passagassawakeag River in the distance. She stayed against him, and he touched the curls. She was so soft and vulnerable.

"You're shivering, Deanna. You must go back."

"No, Aaron. Wait."

She leaned up and touched his mouth with her lips. He held her close again, returning her kiss for a moment before something made him move back.

"We can't be alone, Deanna. It's not a good idea."

"Yes, I know."

Murphy nudged his hand with his wet nose. It was almost as if he was saying, "It's okay; it's going to be okay."

Deanna stepped back. "I shouldn't have said any of that. I'm sorry."

Their gazes met again, and he wanted to tell her how he'd felt that first afternoon when he saw her with the sunlight on her dark curls, how he'd felt she was the most beautiful woman he'd ever seen. He said nothing, but instead whispered, "Never be sorry for expressing your feelings. Feelings are neither right or wrong."

"You aren't moving on?"

"No."

"I. . ." But the words wouldn't come as she turned and ran

in the direction of the house.

Aaron wanted to go after her but knew he shouldn't. Murphy looked at Aaron as if to say, "Well, aren't you coming?"

≈

Long after Aaron returned to the cottage, he felt something amiss in the house but wasn't sure what it was. Then he saw the space in the closet. The wedding dress was gone. When had she taken it? Earlier that day? Yesterday? And why? He glanced around. Everything else in the cottage looked the same. He sat on the bed, head in hands. Could he stay on now, now that she'd said all that? He felt love for her in his heart but couldn't say it. It was too soon. He couldn't commit. There was no way for this to be possible.

Aaron reached deep inside his large duffel bag and pulled out a tattered Bible. He had packed it that long-ago night in Oysterville but until now had not read it.

It still smelled of genuine leather. He looked at his name embossed in gold on the front cover. The Bible fell open to Psalm 34. He read there, "I will bless the Lord at all times: his praise shall continually be in my mouth."

Aaron thought about the things that had happened since he'd left his home. He'd made friends, held several occupations, gone hungry a few times, and was wet and cold on more than one occasion. He'd met Shellie in New York and a woman in northwest Maine at the toothpick factory, but he always left before things got tight. He could do so again.

But he didn't want to leave, and this realization bothered him more than he thought it would. He read more verses by the light of the small lamp beside the bed. It felt good to be in God's Word, and he remembered the times his grandmother had told him Bible stories, the ones he had heard in Sunday school as a boy. He felt the tightness in his chest. Could he run away again? Finally, Aaron closed the Bible and turned down the bed.

ten

Deanna felt like such a fool as she ran in the house and up the steps, hoping her father was still asleep. With tears stinging her cheeks, she peeked in on Maddy. She was angelic as her dark curls fanned her Sleeping Beauty pillow. Matching curtains covered the windows that looked out over the bay.

Leaning down, Deanna kissed her daughter's forehead. Maddy needed a father. Bobby had been a wonderful father, but God took him home and now here she was, acting like a lovesick widow needing a husband and wanting a father for her child. What must Aaron think?

She entered her own room and kicked the boots off. The pink, furry rug felt good to her stocking feet. How she loved this room, the one her mother had lovingly painted the summer before she died. The ruffled curtains were sewn on a Sunday afternoon. The bed was perfect for one or would do for two if they liked to sleep in spoon fashion. *Stop it,* her mind cried out. *You've gotten along just fine so far and will manage longer. If the good Lord wants someone to come along, He'll make sure you see the signs.*

She sat on the edge of the bed, and Aaron's face came to mind. His eyes sparkled when he looked at her as if he cared, really cared. How did one know if they should pursue a feeling or just let it drop?

Dear, Lord, I need direction, big time. Please help me.

Bobby came in a dream that night. In the beginning she dreamed about him a lot, but it had been a long time now. His cocky smile that had warmed her heart in the early days of their relationship seemed to say, "You've got to make a

70

life for you and Madison. Keep me tucked in your heart, but there's room for someone else."

Deanna rose in the morning with renewed hope. She wasn't sure why, but somehow she knew things would work out. She also knew that Aaron was carrying around baggage, something he hadn't shared with her—or anyone else, as far as she knew. What had happened to make a young boy move clear across the United States? It wasn't the usual situation. Kids ran away, yes. She remembered running off to a friend's house once, but when her friend's father said she couldn't live there, she'd returned home, words of forgiveness on her lips. If only Aaron would talk about his life, his childhood. She really knew nothing about him, and it was true what GB had said that first day, "He could be a thief or murderer for all you know. Don't be taken in with his innocent, boyish smile."

Deanna also knew that she was older, by a year or two. Not that it mattered. Well, to some it did. Was that what really troubled him? Somehow she didn't think so.

It was time to put the coffee on and fix breakfast. She hoped Aaron would come in before her father got up. She wanted to apologize for what she'd said. She didn't want to take it back, but something about the look on his face made her know she shouldn't have assumed anything.

But Maddy woke up crying, and after she'd comforted her from what appeared to be a nightmare, Deanna heard her father in the bathroom. The day had begun whether she was ready or not.

ຂ

Aaron had choices. Didn't one always have choices? He could stay here, carry on as if nothing had happened, or he could suggest that Mick find another person to help with the Pound. And yet he couldn't always run off like he had in the past. Didn't there come a time when one faced up to facts? He had to grow up sometime, and maybe that time was now. Maybe Deanna did love him, and it was true he had this overwhelming urge to care for and protect her. And Maddy was a nice bonus in the overall picture. Who got Murphy? He was clearly Deanna's dog, but Mick loved the black lab too.

He dressed and headed for the big house.

Deanna had her back to him when he opened the door. She whirled around, and he saw the hurt look in her eyes. He swallowed hard.

"About—"

"About?"

They both began talking at once.

"I spoke out of turn," she said. "Please ignore what I said."

"I–I. . ." But he couldn't get the words out of his mouth. She wanted to ignore it? She hadn't meant it? Were they just to be friends?

"Okay," he finally managed. He held his hand out. "Let's just be friends then."

The minute the words were out, he realized it was the wrong thing to say. She turned back, but not before he saw her face crumple.

Smoke rose from the fry pan, and she grabbed it, without a pot holder.

It fell to the floor with a resounding crash. "Oh!" she cried out, running to the sink and putting her hand under cold water.

Aaron picked up the cast iron skillet and scooped the bacon back into the pan. Maddy had come into the room and cried at the sight of her mother's crying. Mick bounded out of the bathroom, as much as he could bound, and surveyed the mess in the kitchen.

"What on earth?"

"Oh, Dad, I never burn anything!"

"Nor do you pick up a hot handle! Here, let me see it."

Aaron watched as the older man scrutinized his daughter's burn, and then he was holding her close.

"I—I forgot something at the cottage," Aaron said, wanting to flee as fast as he could. Oh, he'd really solved things now, hadn't he!

"Just a moment, young man." Mick's voice boomed out. Maddy clung to her mother's leg, and Deanna had turned back to the refrigerator for more eggs.

"I don't know what happened here, but you're not moving on again. Not just yet. I believe you signed a rental agreement. . . ."

"Dad!"

But he was adamant.

"I understand," Aaron said. "I'm not leaving, just forgot my gloves on the table."

As Aaron returned to the cottage, he realized he'd really done it this time. Now he was not only an enemy of GB but Mick as well. So much for that inner voice. He'd hurt Deanna, and that was the last thing he wanted to do. He grabbed the gloves and headed back. "Well, God," he prayed aloud, "I'm wanting to listen to You, so You have to tell me what to do now. Do I apologize or what?"

While he waited for an answer, he had work to do, and it wasn't getting any earlier.

eleven

Aaron need not have worried. It was as if nothing had happened. Mick didn't mention the incident, and Deanna smiled and appeared to be fine. Far be it for him to bring it up.

Two days later, Deanna said they had to pick blueberries. "It's now or never. Besides, Dad is doing better."

The drive to Stockton Springs was lovely, with a vivid show of autumn color. "This is my favorite time of year," Deanna said.

"Mine too," Aaron responded.

"Well, I like audumn too," Maddy announced.

They exchanged glances, and Aaron saw the twinkle in Deanna's dark eyes.

The field of blueberry bushes went as far as one could see. Soon they had been assigned an area and started picking.

Aaron couldn't believe how fast Deanna picked. Maddy was like the little girl in her favorite picture book. She ate far more berries than went into the bucket.

"Mommy, are you sure there aren't any bears around here?"

"No, Darling. No bears. We're not in the woods or mountains. Besides, there are too many people picking berries just like we are. People tend to scare them off. Sorry to disappoint you, but no bears."

"We have bears back home," Aaron offered. "One night we heard this clatter-bang and a bear had come right into the garage and overturned the garbage can."

"What did you do?" Deanna asked.

"A big bear?" Maddy asked, holding her hand high over her head.

"No, actually, it was a cub. We started closing the garage door after that."

"I want to hear more," Deanna said, dumping a handful of berries into her nearly full bucket. "C'mon. Tell me another story."

"Yes, tell us a story, Aaron!" Maddy echoed her mother's request.

Aaron put his bucket over for Deanna to help him fill it. He wanted to talk about his family someday, but not right now.

"Please, Aaron." Maddy tugged on his arm.

"Only if you pick more blueberries."

"I will, I will."

"My sister and I went blackberry picking once. Blackberries grow wild everywhere, and they have a wonderful flavor, but the seeds get stuck in your teeth."

"What happened?" Deanna persisted.

"We got lost."

"You did?" Deanna shot him a puzzled look. "But weren't you close to home?"

Aaron chuckled. "Yes, we were, but we went down this old logging road, and it stretched on and on. And then the mosquitoes came, and poor Hannah was eaten alive."

"Who's Hannah?" Maddy asked.

"My little sister."

"Little like me?"

"No, she was older." He looked away, thinking how much Hannah would have enjoyed this excursion.

"So, what did you do?"

"I knew Dad would be worried," Aaron continued, so I stopped at the first house and asked them to call my father."

"Was he mad?"

"Oh my, no. Just worried, because we'd been gone half a day."

"I've never gotten lost," Deanna said.

"Have I been lost?" Maddy asked, popping another blueberry in her mouth.

"No, because I won't let you out of my sight."

Deanna stood and held her bucket up. "With my full one and your half bucket, we'll have enough to last a couple of months at least."

"Yes, we probably better get back to the Pound," Aaron said, dumping his berries on top of Maddy's. "I guess we have to concede that your mother is the best blueberry picker around."

They paid the blueberry grower and headed back.

❧

The following week, the trio, plus dog and a picnic lunch, took another trip, this time to Camden Hills State Park. The scenery reminded Aaron of Leadbetter Point, the northern tip of the peninsula, a place he had explored many times over. He was itching to hike again. It was awesome to be out there alone with his thoughts. He might do the Pacific Crest Trail next. It ran from Mexico north into Canada.

Maddy clapped her hands in the backseat. "We're going on a picnic, a picnic, a picnic!"

"I'd say she's wound up," Deanna said. The car window was down, and Deanna's hair blew in the breeze.

They stopped and got out. The sky was a clear blue, the air warm. Maddy soon shed her jacket and ran around in circles. Murphy ran after a ball Aaron usually kept in his pocket. He turned to take the picnic basket from Deanna.

"I'll find a picnic table," he offered.

"Let's sit on a blanket instead. There's always a blanket in the trunk."

"Okay. Sure."

As the sun hit her hair and face, Aaron suddenly wanted to take her into his arms and just hold her.

"Aaron, do you see yourself going home one day?"

"I don't know." He looked away, not wanting to talk about it, yet wanting her to know. "I have three older brothers. Thomas, Luke, and John. My father held the family together after my mother died by her own hand when I was seven."

"Oh, Aaron, I'm so sorry to hear that. . . ."

"My father shut out happy things. Hugging times. Family picnics. If it hadn't been for my grandparents, we probably wouldn't have had Christmas. Then there was Cora."

"A family member?"

"No. Cora's just, well, Cora. She lives in Oysterville, and when marriage plans didn't work out, she needed someone to care for, so she took us motherless kids on, you might say."

Deanna smiled. "She's the one who made the banana-nut pancakes."

"Yeah, that's right."

Maddy ran up and grabbed Aaron's arm. "Come play Frisbee with me and Murph."

"Maddy, can you wait just a minute?" her mother asked.

Aaron touched her shoulder. "Hey, it's okay. We'll talk again later."

"Promise?"

Aaron crossed his heart. "Yes, promise. Now come on and play with us."

Of course Murphy was the best Frisbee catcher of the four. Sometimes he didn't want to give it up and played tug-of-war.

"I say we eat lunch," Deanna said, "then we can go on a short hike."

"A hike?" Maddy asked.

"Yes, it's like a walk," Deanna explained as she unwrapped sandwiches.

"Oh. Where do we go?"

"Probably down by the water and up through the woods," Aaron said.

"Not that we can keep up with a real hiker," Deanna said.

The lunch was finished in no time, and then they walked along one of the marked trails. Murphy had to be leashed, and he didn't like it, but he had to protect his family. They walked for an half-hour, until Maddy asked to be held.

"Maybe we should go back," Deanna suggested.

"I don't mind carrying her," Aaron said, feeling the little head rest on his chest. By the time they got back to the picnic site, Maddy was asleep. Aaron let Deanna take her and lay her on the blanket.

"I like that little girl," Aaron said. Deanna smiled and shyly took his hand as they sat side by side on the far end of the blanket.

"I know you do, Aaron."

Aaron traced her fingers. They were long and graceful, and he wondered what a ring would look like on her left hand. It could be a ring of hope, because they both had hurts to get over. He pushed the thought out of his mind as fast as it had come.

"Aaron, do you think you might stop running one day? I truly wish you would call your father and tell him where you are. Even if you don't go back—and maybe you don't want to, or maybe you do—but just to let him know that you're alive would be the right thing to do."

He grabbed a blade of grass and tore it into little bits. "I know what you say is true, but I just can't. Not yet."

"You were just a kid when you ran away. Boys do impulsive things. Besides, you were hurting, and it sounds as if there was nobody there for you to turn to."

Aaron pulled away. Deanna didn't know about Hannah. He wondered what she would think then.

Another family came to the small wayside park, and their dog barked when he saw Murphy. Maddy cried out as she sat up and rubbed her eyes. "Where am I?"

"Honey, you're just fine. You're with your mother and me."

He held her close and rocked her in his arms. She laid her little head on his shoulder and closed her eyes, as if aware that no harm would come to her.

Aaron's fingers went through the curls. She was so like her mother. A feeling of wanting to protect her rushed over him.

"Here is your sweater," Deanna said, leaning over. She brushed against his arm, and once again he had to control himself to keep from grabbing her and pulling her down on the blanket.

"I suppose we should head back," Deanna said, as if she had guessed what he was thinking.

"Yes. It's almost three now."

Deanna linked her arm through Aaron's, and he gently patted her arm.

"I suppose if I'm to move on, I need to do it before the first snow flies."

Deanna stopped walking, and the sunshine went out of her smile. "Yes, I suppose you should."

Maddy patted his face. "I love you, Aaron."

He hugged her. "And I love you, Miss Madison."

"Promise me one thing, Aaron," Deanna said then.

"What's that?"

"That when you go back to Oysterville and your life there, that you will remember us and write and let us know how you are doing. That isn't too hard of a promise to keep, is it?"

❧

Aaron wanted to say that he didn't want to go back, that he thought he would miss her too much, but he couldn't say that. She might misunderstand. She might feel obligated into loving him back.

"Of course, we'll keep in touch!"

They trudged back to the car, each with their own thoughts while Maddy chattered on, as if everyone was listening.

The light was on in the Lobster Pound, and two cars were

in the parking lot.

"Are we late?" Deanna asked, looking distressed.

"No, I don't think so."

"I hope Dad's okay."

"Deanna, I think he can handle it. Don't worry."

She gave him a look, as if to say, "That's easy for you to say."

Mick had butter melting in the large pan, had sliced the French bread, and had turned on the water to boil in the huge vat. He glanced up and waved. "So? Was it fun?"

"Yes, Dad. Are you okay?"

"Of course. Why wouldn't I be?"

"We aren't late."

"No, but a car drove in, so I came on down and got things rolling."

In no time Deanna had the plates out, the silverware set in the tray, and napkins stacked on a second tray.

"Was it a good day?"

"Excellent." That came from Aaron. "I know why people love Maine and cannot leave."

Deanna looked up, as if puzzled and wondering if he was referring to the place or the people. She said nothing. She turned toward her father.

"Dad, did you have your nap?"

"Yes, now will you stop your fretting?"

Orders were placed, and the people went to the upper floor, waiting for their lobster.

The night turned out to be more than mildly busy. Most customers were tourists spending the last few days of their autumn vacations.

"We read about this lobster pound and decided to try you out. Did you know there's a review on the Internet?" a family from Kansas asked.

"Is that a fact?" Mick shook his head. "Modern-day technology is something else!"

Aaron had offered to set up the pound with a computer and a better way to keep track of customers, orders, and figures for taxes, if nothing else. He hadn't known much about computers until he worked for the lumber company, and in a week he'd taken a crash course, as they needed to be computerized, but nobody was ready to do it. Aaron, being the last one hired, was elected to learn. And learn he did.

Aaron took two lobsters up to waiting customers, then hurried back down for another pair. It looked like it would be one of those nights when people kept coming in, and they'd use most of the lobsters out of the holding tank. Even though there were other items on the menu, most people wanted lobster. GB was ill and had not gone out since Tuesday; it was now Thursday.

When Aaron came down for at least the tenth time, Deanna reached over and kissed his cheek. "Just because you're so cute."

"Oh, yeah?" He briefly pulled her close with one arm, in a partial embrace, before releasing her and running back upstairs with yet another order.

They made several pots of coffee, emptied out the large ice chest full of sodas, and people still came.

"Must have been the glorious weather. Guess it makes people hungry for lobster," Aaron offered.

"Tail end of the tourist season," Deanna said.

"Some have heard about Deanna's homemade apple pie," Mick quipped.

"Dad! I don't make apple pie for the Pound."

"No, but I've been thinking it would be a good idea."

Aaron laughed, and soon Deanna, seeing the humor, joined in the laugher.

"Actually, it should be blueberry pie, though, not apple. Maine is known for its blueberries. Or maybe cranberry-apple."

"We grow cranberries in Washington State," Aaron said.

"Not as many as you do here, but we're second in the nation."

"I thought you westerners harvested apples, not cranberries," Mick said.

"We do. But cranberries do well near the bay side, not far from where I used to live."

"You going back?" Mick asked.

Aaron removed another lobster from the vat and plopped it on a plate. "I don't know yet."

"You'll always have a job here," Mick said. "Just want you to know that."

And you'll always have a place in my heart, Deanna wanted to say. Instead she quipped, "Yes, you wash down those floors and tables better than anyone we've had."

She then wanted to kick herself for sounding so inane.

"And I appreciate your offer, Mick," Aaron said. "I guess I don't know what I want to be when I grow up."

Maddy, who was in the office and seemingly not paying attention, hopped down from the chair and came over with her opinion. "And when I grow up, I'm going to marry Aaron!"

When everyone laughed, she looked perplexed, as if wondering what she'd said that was funny. It was very real to her.

At nine the neon sign went off, and it was another hour of partial cleanup. As people left, all claiming it was the best lobster they'd ever had, Aaron knew he could be happy here. He'd never had a doubt about it. And he could be happy with Deanna and her child, and yet. . . Talking about his father and his family earlier had made him realize that he needed to take action, needed to talk to his father again, perhaps apologize and start over with a clean slate. That is, if his father were able to forgive him.

There was clam chowder and toast with honey butter for supper. After they'd all eaten, Aaron said goodnight. He needed more sleep than he'd been getting. There were just too many things to think about, and his sleep had suffered.

Soon he'd make up his mind about what to do, and then maybe he'd sleep peacefully.

"Aaron!" Deanna caught him at the bottom of the steps. "It was a wonderful day, and I just wanted to thank you."

"Ditto," he said, taking off his cap and looking in her direction. "We'll do it again. Goodnight."

His heart that had felt lighter suddenly went heavy. Deanna did that. With her sweet smile and kind words he would think of how it would be to have her by his side, working together to perhaps build a house, to share their life, have a child or two to go along with Maddy. But he was in no position to offer her his pledge, his love, or any promises.

Once back at the cottage, he dug out his photo album, which had fallen to the bottom of the duffel bag. Not once had he looked at it in all these years since running off. He knew it was there, and that thought lent him comfort, but he had not been able to look at the photos. Not those of Hannah or of him and Hannah playing in the sand at the water's edge. Not the one, the only one, he had of his mother in a dark suit and a slight smile. She'd been going away that day, his father told him, going to Seattle where she'd start her life over. It had lasted three years before the depression got the better of her and she killed herself to escape, because she really was, in her words, "not a nice person."

Another photo showed the four boys lined up on the deck with trees in the background. There were also photos of his grandparents and a few of his father as a child. And one on his parents' wedding day.

It was his family, his beginning. He belonged there, not here. He would go back. He just had to make enough money to set aside, after paying rent, for a trip to Oysterville. He wasn't sure why it was suddenly clear, but it might have something to do with prayer and how he had asked God for answers.

twelve

Deanna announced Friday morning that she was going out on the boat to check the traps since GB was still ill.

"He should go to the doctor, but he's stubborn like someone else I know," she said. Her father stuck his cherry wood pipe in his mouth and just glared. She invited Aaron to ride along as her sternman. She would empty the traps since Aaron wasn't licensed, but he could help by adding fresh bait. Maddy would stay with Velma Cole from church.

"But I want to go with you," Maddy protested, tossing her coat aside. "It's fun in the boat."

"You'd be totally bored," Deanna said in her firm, no-nonsense voice. "We're going to be out there until past your naptime. You can come another time."

Her lip stuck out. "Promise?"

"Of course I promise. We'll find something fun for you to do. Maybe rent a movie."

They dropped Maddy off, complete with a sandwich, banana, and two cookies in Deanna's old Cinderella lunch box. The little girl ran over to hug Velma Cole.

"We'll be back as soon as we can."

"No problem."

The sun beat down out of a cloudless blue sky, with a few wispy clouds on the far horizon.

"No storm today," Deanna said as they drove back to the Pound and hurried down to the docks. She couldn't help thinking about Bobby, though. Would the fear ever leave her completely?

The *Sylvia Ann*—named for Deanna's mother—bobbed up

and down, as if waiting to be taken out to do her job.

They'd stopped long enough to put on rain gear and hats. Aaron held the boat while Deanna got in, untied the rope, and jumped in.

"Our buoys are green and white with a small ring of yellow. I think GB said there should be about fifty out there."

"Fifty!"

"Several are on one line, you know."

Well, no, he didn't know. Lobstering was definitely different than crabbing.

They jetted across the river and up the bay, wind blowing into their faces. Aaron sat up front with Deanna, thinking how cute she looked, so tiny and almost engulfed by her heavy rain gear. Surely they wouldn't need it today, but she said it was always better to wear it, as it often was blustery and rainy as they went out a ways.

"I think we'll come back with twenty lobsters," Aaron said then. "What do you guess?"

Deanna laughed, pushing a stubborn lock of hair back from her forehead. "I'll say thirty."

"Seems GB has been bringing in an average of twenty, at least since I've been working here."

"That's why we're going to get more, since the traps haven't been checked for a few days."

A row of buoys loomed up in the distance, and Aaron got the pulley and winch ready, but Deanna did the pulling.

"Rock crabs!" she said in disgust. "Toss 'em!"

Aaron threw them back into the water, then baited the empty traps and lowered them back in.

The next one held two baby lobsters. Aaron measured them after Deanna showed him how.

"Too small," he said, tossing them overboard.

The next trap held a female. "Look at the eggs!" Deanna said, pointing.

Aaron looked at the creature's underside, studying the minute particles. There were thousands of eggs.

"She's been marked." She pointed out the notch. "Someone has caught her before and put her back."

"You never keep the female, then?"

"Not us. Some have been known to scrape the eggs off and keep them. If they're caught, it's a heavy fine."

There was only one lobster large enough to keep. It went in the holding bin.

Soon the pots were full of bait and lowered into the water.

"One lobster doesn't look very good."

"We've got a lot more to check."

A boat zoomed past, and Deanna waved. "That's Mr. Pendlebury. He owned a rival pound down the road apiece, but he retired last year and just likes to be out in the water every day."

He waved back as he went back toward the harbor.

More rock crabs were found in two pots, and one trap was broken. "Some conniving lobster figured out how to escape." Deanna laughed. "We'll get him next time! Dad can repair it."

Bottom fish, a huge hunk of seaweed, and a few other miscellaneous fish were caught. On the next to last trap in the string, ten lobsters were legal size, and keepers.

Aaron banded their claws so they wouldn't snap and dumped them into the tank.

"They're vultures. Vultures of the sea," Deanna said, looking back at Aaron.

"When did you first go out on the water?"

They drifted along aimlessly now, the motor humming. "I was probably Maddy's age." She leaned back and gazed overhead. "I can't remember ever not being in a boat. It was more natural to me than riding in the car. The only time we rode in a car was Sunday on our way to church. How about you?"

"I wasn't that young, but I went out on a neighbor's crabbing boat when I was about seven."

Deanna opened the lunch sack and produced two thick meatloaf sandwiches, two pickles, bananas, and chocolate chip cookies. Seagulls soared overhead, swooping down as if expecting scraps.

"Gulls certainly are vultures," Deanna said, throwing her crust in the air.

"That's because you feed them."

"Well, they look pretty the way they zero in on the target."

"And fight over it. . . . Hey, this is the same thing Maddy had."

"I know. That's what was in the refrigerator."

"I love your meatloaf."

"Why, thank you!"

They leaned back and finished their meal. Aaron was missing one thing: his harmonica. Many times he'd wished he had it with him, especially when hiking the trail. Music soothed him. He decided to tell Deanna about oysters.

"It wasn't that way with me. I mean, about growing up on a boat. Oysters are different than crabs or your lobsters. The crabbers go out in a boat; they set the pots and go back later to retrieve them. Oysters grow on strings that have been put down in the water. It's quite a process but not nearly as interesting as going out in the boat every day. You put on hip boots and work when the tide is out. When you come back in from working, you smell to high heaven."

"I guess we had oysters here in Maine once, but lobsters are the thing now."

"How long have you had the Pound?"

"Grandpa got a loan from the government right after World War II, and Dad took over the operation from him."

"And you will take it over next."

Deanna frowned. "I doubt it. GB will have something to say about that."

"What if he doesn't want to lobster anymore?"

"Oh, he will."

Aaron remembered Mick's words but dropped the subject, as apparently Mick had not yet talked to his daughter about his concerns.

"Was your childhood happy?" Aaron asked next.

"Oh my, yes. Very happy, except later on when GB decided he didn't like me."

"You were Daddy's pet."

"And the baby, so I got more attention. My father married late, and Mother didn't think she could have any children. Finally, ten years later, GB comes along. They must have doted on him something fierce. He was eight when I was born, and you know the old saying, 'his nose got cut off.'"

"I had the opposite." Aaron leaned back against a boat cushion.

"Because you were the youngest?"

"Youngest boy, yes. It's not an enviable position, believe me."

"So I've heard."

"Mom had us boys close together, and Dad said she never wanted more than one."

"Why did she keep having babies, then?"

"I have no clue."

"A child should always be wanted," Deanna added.

Aaron nodded. "I couldn't agree more. When my sister Hannah was born, she was so sick, they thought she'd die before she came home from the hospital."

"Really? What was wrong?" Deanna asked.

"Cystic fibrosis."

"Oh, I know a couple from church with a daughter who has CF. We've prayed for the family many times." She touched his arm. "I had no idea, Aaron. I'm so sorry."

"Yeah. Cystic fibrosis is not fun. Some live longer than others, and Hannah did at that, but I don't call it living. Not the way it was the last year before I left."

"You couldn't stay to watch her die. . . ."

It was the first time Aaron had let himself talk about it, but there was something about Deanna that made him open up. She was a good listener. She acted as if she cared. And caring was something he had not had from anyone in Oysterville, not after the trips to Portland stopped. He'd not been in school then, and he enjoyed the time alone with his father. Cora had been kind to him. Cora, who had come to help out after his aunt died, then stayed on.

They finished lunch, and Deanna put the wrappers in a plastic bag. "I think we better be on our way, though I could stay out here the entire day. It's good to be on the water again. Good to drive the boat. And good to have such nice companionship."

"Ditto," said Aaron.

Deanna picked up speed, heading toward the next row of buoys bobbing in the water. The water was still calm, but clouds had moved in across the sky from the north.

"Do those clouds mean a storm?" Aaron asked an hour later as he cleared out the last pot. They now had an even dozen lobsters. There was one more row of pots to check. He couldn't believe it was two o'clock. The time had zipped by so fast.

"I think we'll get some rain, yes, but it's not windy, so I'm heading out for the next batch of traps."

Finally, they hit it big-time. Each trap had at least one lobster that was big enough to keep. "I'm keeping count, and so far we have twenty-five, so we both win," Aaron said.

"Wait! I forgot about one more. GB doesn't always put out this many, but I think I see our buoy in the distance."

They sped to the spot where she'd pointed, and there they were.

"Of course you had to win," Aaron said. "I concede."

"The odds were in my favor." She gave Aaron a playful

swat on the arm. "Besides, I'm the owner."

Aaron didn't want the day to end. If he had his way, he'd be coming out every morning to set and check the traps. He loved the water, the smell of it, the wind in his face, the way the salt water tasted. He would never tire of this job.

"I can see you're enjoying yourself."

"It shows?"

"Oh, yes."

She reached over and took his hand. "I wouldn't mind having you for a fishing partner any day of the week. Too bad GB wouldn't trade off, but he won't. I just know he won't. And you'd need to be licensed, anyway."

"Maybe some day."

"Aaron, you could get licensed, you know. It's something to think about. That is, if you stay. . . ."

Aaron said nothing. He did not know what he was going to do.

"You're a wonderful person," she continued. "You show genuine concern, and you're so good with Maddy. Murph adores you, and my father took to you right off."

"I hope you're pleased with our efforts of the day," Aaron said in an attempt to change the subject.

"Oh, I am." Her eyes lit up. "And how about you?"

"Very much so."

"I think that one lobster may be one of the largest we've ever caught. I'll have to see the measurements in the log Dad keeps."

A sudden wind gust gently rocked the boat; they were about two miles from shore. Deanna glanced to the north, her eyes widening.

"It's a squall. We must have relaxed too long out here."

"I didn't feel it getting cold or anything."

"Neither did I."

She pushed the throttle down, and the boat lurched forward, then stopped.

"Oh, no. Something's wrong." She tried the engine again. Nothing.

"Do you have gas?"

"I'm sure we do. GB fills the tank the night before. Unless he forgot. . ."

Her eyes grew wider. "We've run out of gas before. We'll just need to paddle in, that's all." She handed Aaron an oar.

❧

The outline of the harbor was visible in the distance, and Deanna knew they could make it in before the storm hit if she didn't panic. It was a large craft, but if they both paddled hard, it was possible. She tried not to think about the pending storm and Bobby. But all the terror, the waiting, watching, and praying washed over her now like a giant wave, and she found her mind turning toward God, asking Him to let them return safely.

"Is this what they mean by a nor'easter?" Aaron yelled over the sudden sound of crashing waves.

"Yes!" Deanna yelled back. They were so close, yet made no headway with the paddling. It was as if the tide was pulling them out to sea.

"How about the CB?" Aaron asked.

"The light's off—I think the battery's dead!"

Another huge wave crashed against the boat, soaking them as water splashed over the hull.

"We need to bail," Aaron shouted.

"No!" Deanna shook her head. "Keep rowing. I can't manage both oars. Her arms ached, but she must keep going. She thought of Maddy. Precious little Maddy. "Oh, Lord," she prayed, "please help us to get ashore."

"We'll make it!" Aaron shouted back.

She glanced at him, this young man she barely knew. Was he scared too? *Trust Me,* a voice echoed through her thoughts. *Put your faith in Me. . . .* And she felt her body relax as the fear lifted from her spirit.

"Yes, we're going to make it," Deanna shouted back.

The rain came then, in slanting sheets, just as a light in the distance bobbed toward them.

"Someone's coming to help," Deanna said. Her hands were red and numb from the constant beating of the water.

"You out of gas?" a voice bellowed.

"Yes!" Deanna yelled back, taking a deep breath as another gust of wind hit. "Mr. Pendlebury, you're a godsend."

"I have an extra gas can. I'll try to pull alongside!"

Both boats rocked together, threatening to tear into each other as another gust of wind hit hard, but finally, Aaron grabbed the can. Soon the gas was in the tank, and the boat started right up.

"Phew!" Aaron said with relief.

"Thanks!" Deanna shouted as they headed toward shore—and home.

❧

GB was waiting at the dock, his ample arms crossed, his long raincoat flapping against his legs. "Had a little trouble, I see," he said, shouting against the wind.

"You didn't fill the gas tank!"

"You should have checked," he yelled back. "Or Aaron should have thought of it, since you're a woman and women are known to get rattled."

"Just a minute, GB; that's not fair. I can drive this boat as well as you can, even if I haven't manned it since Maddy's birth."

"Still," he gave her a hand, leaving Aaron to fend for himself. "Still," he repeated, "seems you would remember that was the number-one rule."

"Oh!" She shot past him and on up the ramp. He could be so infuriating. "I'm going after Maddy," she called over her shoulder, shedding her rain gear and reaching for a towel.

Fuming, she sped over the miles to pick up her child. She'd been scared as memories of Bobby filled her mind, yet the water and boating was her whole life. Why hadn't she checked the gas gauge? And why hadn't she seen the storm coming? Life was precious to her now, now that she had a little one to care for. She would not take chances like that again.

Maddy came running when she heard her mother's voice.

"Mommy, your hair is all wet and yucky!"

"I know, Honey. A storm blew in, and we ran out of gas. I thought I'd never feel the hard ground beneath my feet again."

"How about a cup of green tea?" Velma asked. "That should warm you up."

"Tea sounds wonderful." She eased into the nearest chair and pulled her child onto her lap. She caressed the dark curls, loving the feel of her chubby little body. Deanna didn't care if she got back in time to help at the Pound. Let GB do it, along with Aaron and her father. Besides, she didn't want to face GB again with his knowing sneer, his "I can't believe you did that" maddening grin.

"Did this boat problem just happen?" Velma asked, bringing the teapot to the table.

"Yes."

"I knew it," Velma said with a nod. "I felt led to pray around three. I didn't know why, but when God puts something on my heart, I stop whatever I'm doing and just pray."

"Oh, Mrs. Cole!" The tears began again, and this time Deanna let them fall.

The older woman held her close. "There now, you just cry all you want. Tears are cleansing, you know."

"Mommy, what's wrong?" Maddy hopped over and looked into her mother's face. Velma handed her a tissue.

"Mommy's just so glad to be here with you. Don't worry about me crying."

Soon Maddy had a small cup of tea, half cream and a

heaping spoon of sugar. She dipped animal crackers in the tea and said, "Yummy!"

Velma laughed. "Doesn't take much to amuse a child."

"I like it when we have tea, Mommy," Maddy said, hugging her mother. "Oooh, you're still wet and cold."

"That's why I suggested the tea," Velma said. "There's nothing as refreshing as a cup of hot tea."

"But I really do need to go now," Deanna said, pushing her chair back. "What do I owe you?"

"What! You think I'd charge for taking care of my best friend's granddaughter?" Velma's eyes suddenly grew moist. "Oh, but I miss that mother of yours. Sylvia and I did the zaniest things together!"

"Oh, I know—yes, I know." Deanna hugged her hard. "And I miss her so too."

"She'd want you to be happy, Deanna. You know that, right?"

"Yes."

"I think something is going on in your life right now, and I say grab hold and hold on tight."

Deanna wished she could believe Velma Cole's words. If only she knew what Aaron was thinking. If only she could see some sign of affection. His eyes told her he was interested, but nothing ever happened. And even though they were comfortable together—like today out in the boat—she feared it would go no further, and soon he'd be on his way again. She had to wait. What did it say in the Bible about patience? She had lacked it all her life, so maybe it was time she learned.

❧

Aaron was in the open area of the Pound, watching the road, as if waiting for Deanna's car to appear. When she came down the hill, he hurried up and opened the door. "Are you okay? Is Maddy all right?"

"Yes, why do you ask?"

"Hi, Aaron," Maddy called from the backseat as she unbuckled her car seat.

"I thought you'd be right back."

"I was tired and wet and cold and was offered a cup of tea. I hope that was okay."

He stepped back, looking puzzled. "Have I done something wrong?"

And at that question, she turned and hurried up to the house, carrying Maddy like a sack of potatoes.

Why didn't I answer him? she wondered later. Why had she left him standing there with that near hopeless look on his face? Why had she burst into tears before getting into the sanctuary of the house? Why had the day turned out with her feeling stupid and inept? And had GB failed to put in gas on purpose, or did it happen because he'd been ill lately? Maybe she should give him the benefit of the doubt. As for Aaron, she'd apologize for her bad behavior when he came into the house tonight. She hoped he would still come and that he didn't carry a grudge. She couldn't bear for him to be angry with her.

thirteen

"I decided if I ever got through that winter up north logging, I'd be able to survive anywhere."

It was late one night, and Deanna, Mick, and Aaron sat around the fire munching popcorn and halfway watching a news documentary on TV.

"I'd never survive a winter in the wilds," Mick said, moving closer to the fire. "The old bones wouldn't take it."

"Not that you'd ever need to worry about it, Dad." Deanna leaned over and patted her father's hand. The gesture was not lost on Aaron. He liked the way she catered to the old man, because it was done out of love, not duty. He wished, oh, how many times had he wished, for such a relationship with his father.

"I think my days in the wilds of winter are over too," Aaron said, leaning back. "I like the comforts of a nice fire, a full stomach, and being able to put my feet up."

Evenings were often spent talking, reliving the past, as Mick liked to do, and snacking on something Deanna whipped up in the kitchen.

"Never logged," Mick went on. "Always wanted to try it but guess it will have to be in my other life now."

"As if you believed that," Deanna said.

Often the discussions led to religion. Aaron listened while Deanna espoused her faith, her belief in a higher being. Aaron wanted to ask why God allowed tragedies to happen, why he took a young child from a parent's loving arms, why he let a father drown at sea.

"God wants us to lean on Him," Deanna said, as if reading

Aaron's mind. "Oswald Chambers said if there were no valleys, we'd never know the thrill of the mountaintop experience. Things happen because people are disobeying God's laws."

"Hey, I can relate to that mountaintop thing," Aaron said. "That's what I feel when I'm hiking."

" 'Love ye one another,' the second greatest commandment of all," Deanna added

"And love the Lord your God with all your heart, soul, strength and might." Aaron grinned. "Did I get that in the right order?"

"I don't think the order matters that much."

Mick held up his empty coffee mug. "Just a tad more, Honey. It's decaf, right?"

"Of course, Dad."

"Here, allow me." Aaron was on his feet, taking the mug and pouring a bit more for himself as well. Comfort. Ease. Relaxation. He couldn't remember a time when he and his father, brothers, and Hannah had sat around the living room enjoying each other's company. It simply had not happened. Was it because of Hannah's illness? Perhaps it was because they didn't have a mother. But there was no mother here. Mick and Deanna talked, laughed, and debated, yet no cross words were spoken. Mick's voice rose from time to time, but Deanna was calm and collected. He wondered how she did that. Yet he knew she could get angry, remembering the day on the boat.

"How about your family?" Mick asked then, as if he'd been reading Aaron's mind. "What did you do of an evening?"

"Nothing like this," Aaron said. "We weren't into discussing things. We each went our own way. Hannah needed lots of attention, especially in the last few years of her life, so Dad spent every moment doing for her."

"And your mother?"

"My mother left the family when I was four or so. She's dead now."

"Oh, Lad, I'm sorry to hear that."

Aaron drained the last of his coffee and rose to his feet. "Suppose I'd better get back to my place." He caught Deanna's glance and nodded. He didn't want to leave, but sometimes you had to do what you had to do.

⁂

Long after Aaron left and her father had gone to bed, Deanna sat in the semidarkness, wondering why Aaron was uncomfortable when talking about his past. Everyone had problems, and nobody was perfect. And sickness was rampant, at least in the families she knew. If he could just talk about it, he might feel better. He claimed to believe in God, but his actions didn't always show it. He was troubled, and she wanted to ease the pain if he'd just let her get close.

Still, thoughts of getting close to Aaron made her breath come in fast gulps. This felt different from how it had been with Bobby. Bobby had been her first love, and somewhere Deanna had read that first loves were unique. She was older now and, she believed, wiser. She was a mother and had been a wife; she worked hard. Her life had been good. The one thing she lacked, the thing she wanted more than anything, was to find someone with whom to share those precious moments, someone to trust and confide in, someone to love and to love her back. Was it going to happen one day?

She picked up the framed photo of her parents on their twenty-fifth anniversary, which was shortly before her mother's death. Even then the cancer was working on her, but she did not know it. Her mother looked so young and beautiful. Deanna had been only fifteen; GB was twenty-three. She wasn't one to complain, just as her father wasn't.

"You have your mother's gentle ways," her father often told her. "You're also pretty, but not as pretty as my Sylvie was.

Nobody has ever been that pretty."

Her mother was a New Hampshire girl who had come to Maine on vacation. She had met Mick at the Lobster Pound, where she and her family had a meal. Mick, fresh out of the Navy after a six-year stint, ran it with his father, who had also been a Navy man.

"I knew from the moment she first smiled at me that she was the one. I had to wait, though. She was too young, lived too far away. But we corresponded. And I was like a 'smitten puppy' as my father said."

Deanna never tired of hearing the story. She remembered Grandfather Nelson also, though he had died when she was ten. She wondered what it would be like to wait five years for the person you loved. Could she wait five years for Aaron? Would it take him that long to find what he was searching for? Would he want to take her along, to be yoked with him for the rest of his life? She could settle for nothing less.

"You like him, don't you?" her father had said the second day after Aaron arrived. "I can tell, you know."

"Dad, he's such a nice man, but I honestly don't know what I feel right now."

"Don't hide your feelings, Child. Go as the Lord leads you. He's guided you before, and He'll guide you again."

Deanna wondered why the words haunted her now. What she wanted was to bundle up and go for a walk, but she wasn't prepared to run into Aaron again. She put her feet up on the coffee table, thankful that Aaron had stumbled onto the Nelson Lobster Pound. God had led him here; she believed it with her whole heart. And God would turn his life around; she was positive of that too.

The last flame went out, with only the embers remaining. It made her think of her heart and how it felt right now. Bereft, without Bobby. But Bobby was gone. It was time to move on, time to build another fire, just like this fire would be rekindled tomorrow evening. A passage of Scripture from the third chapter of Ecclesiastes came to mind: *"To every thing there is a season, and a time to every purpose under the heaven. . . . A time to weep, and a time to laugh; a time to mourn, and a time to dance."*

She had wept when her mother died and again when Bobby drowned. There had also been happy times. She'd beamed with pride when her newborn had been laid in her waiting arms. She'd laughed when her baby first recognized her face, when Madison heard her name and smiled, when she walked and talked and her hair turned curly. Mourning came with the deaths, but after mourning was a time to dance, a time to move on. Yes, it was time for her. Was it going to be time for Aaron as well?

Deanna looked back at the embers and took the cups to the kitchen. Enough time spent on memories.

❧

Aaron wondered if God had put these thoughts about Deanna in his mind. He liked the way her eyes lit up when he entered the room.

The cottage was cold, but he didn't turn on the heat. He'd clean up and go to bed. Tonight he wanted to read Scriptures. There was something she'd said that he wanted to see if he could find. He remembered hearing the verses before, something about everything in its own time. He wondered where he'd find it. He should have asked her. Somehow he knew she would know exactly what book it was in.

He read a few Psalms, deciding he'd do the search tomorrow. And maybe he'd just ask Deanna, swallow his pride, and show his difficulty with remembering Bible verses. That was okay, wasn't it? Not everyone could remember where to find what. The Bible was a huge book. His mother hadn't believed, or she wouldn't have done what she did. His aunt had told him that people were never in their right minds when they committed suicide. Was that true? He wished he could remember more about his mother, but the main thing was the constant weeping. He could hear her, as his bedroom was directly below his parents' room. Loud voices always sounded before the crying began. Sometimes his father would leave, and Aaron would hunker down, wondering where his father was going and wishing he had stayed. Wishing his mother would stop crying. And wishing he wouldn't waken to hear Hannah crying, then coughing— always coughing.

The brothers, being older, worked in the oysters, and Aaron remembered going down to the bay when he was six or seven and being shown how to do it. He'd never liked the work, always wishing he could be in one of the crabbing boats that went up the bay to set out their pots. Why hadn't his father chosen that kind of work? It wasn't as messy.

Of course he hadn't known then that crabbing was messy too. And hard work. Still, it was his dream to one day own a boat, to be respected as an upstanding member of the community. And if it happened, how would his father react? He knew his three older brothers didn't care. Nobody really did, so why should he return to Oysterville?

He thought of Cora, who had tried to be a mother. She'd be there when he returned from school, offering him a plate of cookies and a glass of milk. He also saw how she watched his father and had a feeling that Cora was there, not because of the kids, but because of Leighton. He wondered if his father even knew. And was she still there taking care of things, running the house and cooking meals, keeping the cookie jar full? He imagined she probably was.

He closed the Bible, glad he'd brought it, though he hadn't read it much in the past few years. Could he ever have a strong faith like Deanna and her father? Was that what gave them such peace, made them rely on, love, and care for each other? Was it what put the smile on Deanna's lips? What made her work hard and take care of things, then begin the whole process over again the next day? Faithful. That was a word to describe her. She was faithful to all—her God and her family.

He opened the curtain and looked out into the inky darkness. He liked the cottage. He wondered how the young couple had managed. It seemed small for two, but when you're in love, you want to be close. Would he ever find closeness or such solace?

fourteen

Mick announced one day in early November that he had decided to follow Aaron's earlier suggestion and get the Pound computerized.

GB protested. "Dad, we've been getting along just fine without it; why add an extra expense now?"

"What's wrong? Are you afraid you'll lose some of your inheritance?"

"Dad! That's not fair."

"Well, it's the truth, isn't it?" He chewed on his beloved pipe. "I want to go forward, and it bothers you. I say it's because Aaron suggested it. Right? Why don't you like him?"

"He's a no-account drifter."

Mick tapped his pipe on his boot. "He may be a drifter, but I dare say 'no-account' is way too harsh."

"What do you know about him?"

"That he's honest. I know he's a good, hard worker, and that he's from the West Coast—a place called Oysterville."

"Why isn't he back there, working in the oysters, then?"

"That part I don't know."

GB shook his head. "Dad, it's going to cost you."

"I know that, Son. But we can get a Web site and take orders with the computer, and it sounds like a great idea. It isn't as if I just jumped in with both feet. Been thinking about it for several weeks now."

"Whatever. I'm going home."

Deanna was pleased when her father and Aaron came home with the computer. They'd gone to Bangor and looked around for the best deal.

"Right now we just need to get this baby set up."

"There's a desk up in the spare bedroom. I think the two of us can handle it."

They carried the desk down and set it in a corner of the living room.

"I'll work on this tonight," Aaron said. "Won't take long to get you going. Then I'll give you both lessons."

Mick held up his hand. "I don't want a thing to do with it. Never liked machines."

"Now, Dad, you need to learn too."

"I'll leave that up to you young folks."

Maddy was more excited about the large box she now had to play with. She crawled in with her favorite bear and blanket. "It's a playhouse," she called out. "Can I color on it and make windows?"

Deanna laughed. "Of course."

Aaron had the computer up and running a few hours later.

"How do you know about computers?" Mick asked.

"I learned at one of my jobs. They had a computer, and I studied manuals and picked it up. Soon people were asking me to fix computers and printers."

"It's the up and coming thing for sure," Deanna said, sitting down and admiring the colorful screen saver. Maddy was enthralled with the bright colors in all sizes and shapes that kept moving about on the screen.

"I could look at this all day," Deanna said.

"And later on, if you want a change, I can put a photo of Maddy on it."

"You could?"

"Sure. It would be neat, I think."

Deanna learned the first few things she needed to know in order to use the computer—how to sign on and where to find different programs.

"It isn't a play thing," Mick humphed when he saw the Solitaire game on the screen.

"No, it's not. But she needs to learn how to use the mouse, and this is a good way to practice."

A few days later, they had an E-mail address, and the Web site was up and running. Now all they had to do was wait for orders to come in.

There were three orders the following morning. Deanna was impressed. "We might not be able to keep up with this, Dad. Here's an order from Oregon. Can you imagine? A business in Portland, Oregon, wants our lobsters."

GB had to go into the house and see the computer the next day. "Why isn't it in the office?" he asked. "Seems that is where you'd want it."

Deanna shrugged. "Maybe not. It's less damp and cold in the house. I can process orders and things after we close at night."

GB just stared at the screen.

"Here, you want to try?" Deanna urged him.

"Nah. I don't like computers. I don't like cell phones and all this other modern stuff." He turned and barreled out the door.

Aaron showed Deanna how to play another game that night. He told her to beware, because she could get hooked on it. Mick grunted from his easy chair. "Maybe GB's right. Seems this could be a boon, but it could also boomerang."

During the next few days, Deanna explored chat rooms, different Web sites, and e-mailed her cousin in New Hampshire. One day the Missing Persons link piqued her interest, as she hoped to find an old school friend, Lois Ann.

If Aaron hadn't set up the computer and included his name as one of the contact people, there never would have been a message from Courtney Spencer. Deanna stared in disbelief at the words on the screen:

*I am seeking a young man named Aaron Walker. He
just turned twenty-two. He comes from the West
Coast—Washington State to be exact—a small town
called Oysterville. Aaron knows a lot about oysters, as
his father is an oysterman. He might mention having
three older brothers and a sister who died of cystic
fibrosis.*

*He is medium height, has sandy blond hair, and is a
friendly sort. If you have any info, please contact me at
this E-mail address.*

Deanna felt fear rush over her. Fear like she always felt when
she thought Aaron might move on. This Courtney had to be an
old girlfriend. How else would she know this much about him?

Deanna stared at the message, reading it through two and
then three times. She had to tell Aaron. He was at the Pound,
getting it ready for tonight's customers. What would he do?
Would he pack everything and get out of East Belfast first
thing in the morning? What if she didn't tell him? He'd never
know. How would he? He left most of the computer work up
to her. She took the orders, answered questions, and was
enjoying learning about chat rooms and other items of interest. Why had she gone into the Missing Persons link?

Deanna shut off the computer, doing it the way Aaron had
showed her, and went upstairs to check on Maddy. The child
clutched her bear tight, and the sight of her daughter caused a
knot to rise in Deanna's chest. She should never have planned
or considered about how it would be if Aaron were to stay, if
Aaron fell in love with her, if Aaron would give up his earlier
life and be content to stay here. The idea had crossed her
mind many times in the weeks since Aaron came. And
Maddy loved him. Murphy loved him too. The big dog loved
playing ball and being scratched. Mick had come to rely on

the hardy young man. Only GB would rejoice if Aaron left. And leave he would if she told him about this Courtney. Maybe she could bring up the name casually and see if there was any reaction.

Deanna had never been devious in her life. Honesty was her middle name. Once, when a boy had shown interest in her, she'd refused to go out with him because her best friend liked him. No, she had to tell him. But perhaps she could wait a bit longer? That was deceptive, but not totally so. Yet all the while it was as if God was telling her she had to tell him, that it was important that someone reach him. It might not be a girlfriend after all.

Deanna bundled up Maddy when she finally awakened— a jacket and a scarf to keep the wind out of her ears. The wind was fierce this afternoon, and Maddy was inclined to get earaches.

Aaron was readying things in the serving area. "I think we're ready. Doubt that we will have any customers coming in from boats tonight. At least I wouldn't want to be out in this wind."

"I hope GB gets back soon."

"That's right. Shouldn't he be here in ten minutes or so?"

Deanna nodded. She had Maddy go to her little corner to play. Deanna was lucky that Maddy was such a good, cooperative child. She wondered if she ever had a boy, if he'd be mild and quiet like this. She also wondered if he'd have sandy blond hair and ruddy cheeks, or would he be dark-haired like her?

She couldn't not say anything. She just couldn't.

"Do you know someone named Courtney?"

Aaron stopped polishing the counter and glanced over. "Courtney? No, I don't believe so. Why, does someone named Courtney know me?"

A bit of relief went over her. She wasn't a past girlfriend. His face would have given him away. That was one thing she knew about Aaron, had known from that first day. Like her, he was honest. He could not outright lie; she was sure of it.

"Her last name is Spencer."

It was then that Deanna realized Courtney hadn't said where she was from. She could be from anywhere, be anyone. Just someone who liked to surf the net. Yet if this resulted in Aaron going home, returning to Oysterville, it might as well be a girl. He'd pack in a minute and be gone by morning's first light.

"Why do you ask?" Aaron repeated. He stood watching her, as if wondering what was wrong. "Who is this Courtney, and what does she have to do with me?"

She avoided his steady gaze. "You'd better go up and find out for yourself. She left a message on the computer, at the Missing Persons' site."

"She did? You mean someone, after all this time, has actually tracked me down?"

"Maybe she's been there all along—you just never went to the right place on the Internet."

"I suppose I need to go see about it."

He was off up the hill, throwing a ratty old ball for Murph as he went. Deanna swallowed back the tears. It couldn't be good news. It just couldn't. She hoped he'd find out soon. What if it was about his father—maybe he was dying and needed Aaron? She couldn't try to hold him here then. Fathers were important. She knew how she'd feel if something happened to her father.

Maddy showed her the picture she'd drawn, and Deanna broke down and cried.

The little girl looked up, her hand touching her mother's cheek. "Mommy, is my picture making you sad?"

"Oh, no, Honey." She cried even harder as she clutched her

close. "It isn't you, Sweetie. It's just something else. Mommy doesn't feel very good."

That was true. Her stomach churned, and there was a pain, the pain of loss, in her heart. No way could she tell Maddy that her reason for tears was because she had drawn a small child at a table, a mother, and a father, and they were holding hands as they bowed their heads to say grace. A family. That's what Maddy wanted and needed: a real family.

❧

Aaron turned on the computer and went to the Internet. Five minutes later, he found the message. His breath stopped. Someone named Courtney was looking for him. He didn't know how old the message was or why she was looking for him, but it could be anything. My father. His mind went to Leighton, and he wondered if he could have had a stroke or a heart attack. He sat back, drumming his fingernails on the desktop. He had to find out.

He went into E-mail, typed in the address, and sent a message.

> *I don't know who you are, Courtney, but I am Aaron Matthew Walker, and I am from Oysterville. What does your message concern? Is it about my father, Leighton Walker? I'll give you the phone number where I am staying. I'm in Maine. Do call and let me know. Thank you—*
>
> *Aaron Matthew Walker*

There certainly could be more than one Aaron Walker, but he doubted that there would be another Aaron Matthew Walker. He waited a full minute before hitting "Send," then his message was on its way.

He turned the computer off and went back down the hill to

the Lobster Pound. Strange how one day your life is one way, and you get up the next morning and it all changes. Of course he might not return to Oysterville. He liked it here. When Deanna asked about Courtney, he knew she feared it was an old girlfriend, but he honestly had never known anyone named Courtney.

Deanna glanced up, a look of mixed emotion on her face. "Did you find the message?"

Aaron nodded. "I'm sure it was someone who knows my father. I don't know anyone with that name."

"Maybe he hired her to search for you."

He shrugged. "Could be, I guess." But inside, he asked, Why did it take him so long? And yet, maybe he has been searching all along.

"I sent a message back, so we can check later tonight or in the morning."

"I hope it's nothing serious."

"So do I, especially since my car won't make it that far, and I don't have enough money for airfare."

"My father would loan you the money. I know he would."

"Let's just see if this Courtney answers tomorrow."

It wasn't an E-mail message but a phone message on the answering machine awaiting them when they went up the hill to have a late supper.

Deanna pushed the button as a man's deep voice filled the room.

"Aaron, is this the right phone number? Is this my son, Aaron Walker? I am confused, because the recorded message said something about a Lobster Pound. I'm looking for someone named Aaron. Are you there, Little Buddy?"

Aaron jumped to his feet and looked out the window. It was his father, all right. His voice hadn't changed a bit. He balled his fists at his side while the message went on—something about coming home and missing Aaron.

"Here's the number," Deanna said, handing him a sheet of paper.

"Thanks, but I do remember my own phone number. Nothing changes much in Oysterville, especially not phone numbers." He didn't have to look to know that she was chewing on her lower lip.

"Are you going to call?"

"Of course."

"Why don't you use the phone upstairs so you have privacy?"

"Thanks. I will."

Of course Maddy wanted to go up too, but Deanna put her arm around her. "Aaron has to make an important phone call, Honey." Even as she said it, she felt the tears threaten again. It could be the phone call that would change her life.

ॐ

The phone rang just once and then was picked up.

"Hello."

Aaron swallowed hard. "Dad? It's me, Aaron. Your Little Buddy."

"Oh, my. Alice was right. She said you'd call."

"Alice? Who's Alice?"

"A friend whom I hope you will meet if you come home. Her daughter Courtney thought about the Internet search. I didn't think it would work."

So that's who Courtney is. But who is Alice? "Dad, I have a job here."

"I figured as much."

"I'd like to come, but well, I can't just up and quit."

"Of course you can't."

"I want to see you."

"Oh, Aaron, how about Thanksgiving? Could you come to see me then?"

Aaron wondered how he could tell his father he had no money. Well, he couldn't. He just couldn't. As it turned out, he need not have worried.

"I'll send the money for a ticket. You find out the cost, and the money will be there."

"Dad, are you sure?"

"Never more sure of anything in my whole life. It's been too long, Son. We have some fences to mend."

"Yes, Dad, we do."

Aaron sat on the edge of Mick's bed and wondered what he would say. He knew the old man would understand, since he was a father. He wasn't sure about Deanna, but it was GB who would rub it in now. "See? I told you he was just a drifter. Well, good riddance, I say!"

Aaron walked back down the steps, listening to the sound of the late news on the TV and the clicking of keyboard keys while Deanna left a message for someone. He walked in and cleared his throat.

"Looks like I'm going to be heading back to Oysterville for Thanksgiving."

"Going to see your family?" Mick asked, looking away from the TV.

"Yes, to see my family."

"Who is Courtney?" Deanna had to know who this woman was who had turned her life upside down.

"She's the daughter of a friend of my father's, and she was certain she'd find me on the Internet."

"And she did." Deanna looked away. "One thing I know for certain," she said, "is that there is going to be one very disappointed little girl when you leave and one unhappy black lab."

"And I believe there's someone else who will feel the same way, though she won't admit it," Mick said.

"Dad!" Deanna's cheeks flushed pink.

Aaron knew she couldn't let him know what she really thought now, how she didn't want him to go. He wanted to tell her that he didn't want to go, either, yet hearing his father's voice had taken away some of the hurt, and he found himself eager and curious. Would his brothers be glad to see him, or would he be like the prodigal son, with the father eager to have a big feast while the boys resented all the attention he might get? It could be interesting. And yet, in spite of all the possible consequences, he found himself needing to find out, wanting to go home at last. Home to Oysterville. . .

fifteen

The trip across country was uneventful and definitely took less time than Aaron's cross-country trip to Maine that began five years earlier. This was his first flight. There'd never been a reason to fly before. He liked all of it except taking off.

"Thanks for flying with us today," a flight attendant said as she pointed out the safety measures. Something about her smile made him think of Deanna. Not that he'd ever stopped thinking about her. He really hadn't thought he would react this way. Her face, her smile, the way she touched his arm, haunted him, and he'd thought of little else during the flight.

❧

Deanna had insisted on taking him to the Bangor airport. "No way am I going to let you take the bus there."

"I could, you know."

She sighed. "Of course you could, but I have to see you off."

They talked constantly on the forty-five-mile trip. Impersonal but important things. Such as, if he ever came back, he'd have a job. He knew that. Then they were there, and he told her to go home because she couldn't come down to the waiting area anyway, not with all the security measures now taken at airports.

"Promise to e-mail me," she said as he got his bag out of the trunk.

"I doubt my father has a computer, but I'll write," he called over his shoulder.

She suddenly was out of the car and running toward him. "Aaron, I'm praying for a time of forgiveness, for you to be one with your family again. We'll all miss you, you know."

Then he was kissing her and grabbing her for a longer kiss

114

before leaving to enter the airport terminal. His last glimpse was of her waving and blowing him a kiss.

❧

Aaron closed his eyes in an attempt to sleep. It didn't work. He then read the airline's magazine and ate the breakfast they brought, a muffin that tasted like cardboard.

He looked out over the wing of the plane. The late fall day was clear, then they went in and out of clouds. It was like magic. It became clear again, and he saw farmlands flatter than he could have ever imagined, then they passed over the snow-covered Colorado Rockies, Mount Adams in Washington State, and then Oregon's majestic Mount Hood. They started the descent to land at Portland International. Would his father and brothers be there to meet him?

The landing took forever, but finally they were on the tarmac and taxiing to the gate.

Soon people popped up, retrieving their luggage from the overhead bins. Aaron had checked in his one bag, as it was too large to fit under the seat or overhead. Though unencumbered by luggage, he let others exit ahead of him. They seemed to be in such a rush. Maybe he should have been too, but he just wasn't. There was this inner fear that his father would still be angry, that nothing would be resolved.

When he finally got up to the baggage area, a large sign greeted him, and a huge cheer went out: WELCOME HOME, AARON!

A sea of faces enveloped him, and then he felt his father's hug as he was pulled into the older man's grasp.

"I can't believe my Little Buddy has come home."

"Aaron, glad to see you again!" It was his brother, Luke, and children surrounded him. How many kids did he have, anyway?

"Son, I want you to meet Alice, my wife."

Aaron looked into the face of a laughing woman, and he held her proffered hand.

"Dad? You didn't tell me you were married."

"I wanted it to be a surprise."

Aaron was surprised, all right. As far back as he could remember, his father had never dated. Not once. Now here he was married. The warm smile made him feel good, though.

"Courtney, my daughter, the one who found you on the Internet, couldn't make it. Steven Carl, the baby, takes up a lot of time, but she'll be at the house, and we're having a big celebration tonight."

House? What house? They weren't heading for Oysterville now?

Aaron moved with the throng. The contingency was seven people. His father, Alice, his brothers—all three, and two of Luke's children. The wives had stayed home, for what reason, Aaron didn't know. And soon he would meet Courtney, Steven, Courtney's husband, and their baby. It was mind-boggling. To go from having nobody to suddenly belonging to a family again was going to be mighty strange.

Alice's house had been explained to him on the trip. She and his father lived in Portland part of the year, and the rest of the year they lived in Oysterville. That part alone was hard to imagine.

Aaron waited, knowing someone would ask the inevitable question: Why did you run off like that? But so far, nobody had. His brothers drove their vehicles, while he rode with Leighton and Alice.

"We have a wonderful dinner prepared. We will stay here for the night, then go home to Oysterville tomorrow morning," Leighton said.

"I want to e-mail Deanna—let her know I arrived okay."

"Deanna?" Both Leighton and Alice echoed the question.

"Yes, she's the daughter of the man who owns the Lobster Pound where I work. We're just friends."

Leighton and Alice exchanged glances but said nothing.

"Your father and I used to e-mail each other several times a day," Alice said then, playfully hitting her husband's arm. "It's the best way ever to keep in touch."

He didn't write when they first arrived at the house because it was pandemonium. He met Courtney, who had sent the E-mail message, and Steven, who owned a computer business, and got a glimpse of the baby. It was almost too much to comprehend.

"I need to send that message," Aaron said after a dessert of chocolate cake topped with vanilla ice cream. Apparently his father remembered his fondness for chocolate.

Aaron sat in front of the blank screen for a long moment. Why was this difficult? Why was he experiencing this sinking feeling when he thought of what Deanna must be doing now? Because of the three-hour time difference, she would have Maddy in bed and would be in front of the computer playing a game, sending a message to one of her old friends, or sitting in the darkness. He doubted that she'd find his message until tomorrow.

Deanna,

I arrived on time to find a throng of people with a silly sign welcoming me home. I didn't quite know what to say.

My father is married, and that was a shock. It'd be like your father suddenly getting married. You probably wouldn't know how to handle it. I'm having a problem with it, although Alice is nice, and my father seems happy. Alice has a daughter and a grandchild, so I have more than one to get acquainted with. Courtney, her daughter, is the one who first wrote.

As I sit here alone in this room, with noise pouring out from the living room and family room, I find myself wanting to be back in Maine, where it's quiet.

Just wanted to let you know I am fine. Hope you are the same. You can write to me if you want.

❧

Deanna had checked her E-mail every ten minutes, hoping, oh so hoping, that Aaron would write. Her father had shut off the TV at ten, saying she was silly to expect him to keep in touch.

"I love you, Daughter, but sometimes you're not too smart when it comes to men."

"Dad, you don't know that. Aaron and I have something special. I believe with all my heart that God brought him here to us. He went home because he has some things to clear up, but I think he's coming back." A tear slid down her cheek. How could he forget their kiss? It sealed her thoughts and feelings for him, and she knew he had responded with the same. *At least that's what I'm praying,* she thought.

"See you in the morning," her father called, his footsteps clattering up the stairs. "I know the time is different there, but I wouldn't wait up too much longer for a letter." Deanna ran after him to give him a big hug. Above all, she wanted him to know that she loved him. After all, he was the only sure thing in her life, the bit of stability she needed.

The letter came at eleven P.M., Maine time.

She read it twice, looking for some small sign that Aaron missed her, that he maybe even loved her. He said he missed the quiet. That she could believe. He said she could write, if she wanted.

If? Wild horses couldn't keep her from writing back. But she'd be careful. She couldn't give away her heart and what she felt. She had done so once, and Aaron had not reciprocated. She would not make that mistake again.

Aaron,
  You have no idea how glad I am to hear from you. I knew there would be a bunch of people to meet you. That's the way families are. Sometimes I miss having a big family, people to get together with for holiday dinners.

But I have Dad and Maddy, and that's enough for now.
Dad's gone on to bed, and Maddy has been down for
quite some time. Murph is looking for you. I could tell
when I came out of the house just before opening the
Pound. He kept looking at the door, as if waiting for you
to come, then stared down the path, thinking you might
appear. If dogs could talk, he'd say he misses you!

Do write again. I want to know how Oysterville looks,
and all your old haunts, old girlfriends, etc.

Your good friend,
Deanna

She had to put in the part about girlfriends—let him know
that she was aware there were other women vying for his
love. She wanted to tell him, "Oh, how I miss you," and sign
her letter "All My Love," but that wouldn't be right. Aaron
had to come to grips with his life, what he'd run away from.

Deanna shut off the computer, then the lights, and tiptoed
up the stairs. Her steps were not bouncy, for she wished that
someone was going with her. Someone, she realized now,
whom she loved with all her heart and soul. Not that she hadn't
loved Bobby, for she had, but Bobby was gone, and she
needed to get on with living. "Life is for the living," her
father had said more than once.

She thought again about Aaron's letter. His father had married, and Aaron truly seemed shocked, yet wasn't that part of
God's plan—that people would find each other and live
together in harmony? But one needed to find someone they
could be equally yoked with.

The bedroom looked as it always did, but for some reason
she felt lonelier tonight. She wanted to be with Aaron now,
wanted to meet his family, wanted to be in a loving family
circle. Dare she hope that this might become a reality some
day, or should she give up her dream and just get on with it?

She sat at her window bench and picked up her journal. There were several entries, all added since Aaron first came looking for a job.

"Do I lose hope, or do I hang on to what I dream about, what I believe and want and truly think might happen someday?"

A moon slid behind the layer of clouds, and Deanna closed the journal. Far away a young man sat with his family, and she couldn't help the tears that came and coursed down her cheeks. She just wanted him to be happy. That was the main thing. . . .

◆

Aaron was given the guest room and left the party early. He was on eastern time, after all. He hadn't slept on the plane, though he'd thought he might, and last night had been a no-sleeper. *Deanna.* Why did her face keep popping into his mind? She had her life in Maine, and he would have his here. A crabbing boat was what he wanted. He'd do crabbing rather than oyster harvesting. He hoped his father would agree.

He pulled back the comforter, wondering if Deanna would find his message. Tomorrow he would check, but for tonight he would merely dream of her last impulsive hug, the way her lips had touched his, lightly at first, then with fervor. "Do come back as soon as you can. You will always have a job with us! Dad wanted me to tell you that."

"And I love you," Maddy had said before he left the house, throwing her arms around his legs. He'd lifted her high, and then held the child tight. He had wanted to include Deanna, but she was looking out the window. He saw the tears before she turned away and knew she was crying silently now. But what could he do? He had to go, had to return to Oysterville. If he went back, he would go to her; he would let her know how he really felt. If, if, if. . . It was a short word but had such deep meaning. . . .

sixteen

The peninsula, this little corner of southwest Washington State, had changed. Aaron looked for familiar landmarks as his father drove through the town of Long Beach. Being a resort area, the usual entertainment area was intact: the merry-go-round, bumper cars, the Game Center, Cottage Bakery, then gift shops, restaurants, and pharmacy on the corner by the light. Gone was the Book Vendor, where he had gone to pick up his girlfriend Jill, who worked there on Saturdays.

"What happened to the bookstore?" he asked.

"Well, the owner wanted an art store to go in there, so that's what happened."

"No bookstores?"

"Oh, sure. There's still Sandpiper Books in the mall."

Alice turned around. "I imagine it seems strange to come back after five years."

Aaron nodded. He wanted to like her; she seemed nice, but it was going to take getting used to, her being his stepmother. He had heard the story of how they met when his father took a laptop in to be fixed. Alice worked in her son-in-law's office a few days each week and was there when Leighton came to pick up the laptop. One thing led to another, then she'd come to Oysterville for a visit, and that was that.

Deanna came to mind again. She was already getting ready for the evening's customers by now. He could see her bobbing back and forth, her dark hair dancing as she waited on each one and wished them, "Bon appetite!"

"Did you meet anyone in Maine? Besides Deanna?" Leighton

121

asked, breaking through his thoughts. *How uncanny,* Aaron thought. It was as if his father were reading his mind.

"A few girls."

That answer was as good as any. He didn't care to discuss any of the women he'd met while traveling—especially not Deanna.

"Jill is single," Leighton said. "Just ran into her at the store last Sunday after church."

Aaron had thought at one time he might marry her. He'd been just a kid then, not even sixteen, but had wanted someone to love, someone to love him. Like most teenagers, Jill had not been ready to settle down and apparently still was not ready to settle down.

"She was married briefly to Lenny. Remember the kid who used to work for us on Saturdays?"

"Lenny?" Aaron tried to put a face to the name but couldn't.

"He left the peninsula shortly after the divorce. I have no idea where he is, but Jill is at Jeanine's, working part-time. It's close to winter, so things have slowed down a bit."

"How's the clamming?" Aaron asked then.

"We were open last month and the first part of November. People been getting their limit."

"I can't wait to see the house," Aaron said as they drove through Ocean Park on their way to Nahcotta. Then it was a straight shot down Sandridge and home.

"And Jolly Roger's is still canning oysters, I bet."

"Oh, yeah. Think the owner will retire soon, though—leave it to others to run."

"Just like you are doing," Alice said. She turned, and their eyes met briefly as the car headed north.

The huge Monterey Cypress trees still stood like sentinels, forming a canopy high over the road. But a lot was cleared by Morehead Park, and the old barn was gone.

"What happened to the barn, huh, Dad?"

"Oh, they had to raze it. Just too dangerous to leave up without doing major repairs."

He was almost home. Home. The thought brought back memories, some painful. That last night here, with Hannah coughing on and on, his father hollering at him to just leave, to go away. And then his footsteps going to her room. He wasn't needed to help. Hannah's last words had been, "I'm going to be okay, Aaron," said between bouts of coughing.

Yeah, right, he'd thought. *When pigs can fly on the moon.*

He put the idea out of his mind. It was no good going over it. Heaven knows he'd gone over it repeatedly since that night. Five years' worth of remembering, wondering, and wishing it had been different. Wishing he'd just stayed.

And yet, he wouldn't have met Deanna if he had.

"We're getting close, Little Buddy." Leighton put his arm around the back of the car seat and touched Alice's shoulder. It was these little acts of endearment that bothered Aaron, yet he knew this was silly; the problem was, he could not recollect a tender aspect to his mother and father's relationship.

Piles of oyster shells dotted the landscape, and then they were past Joe Johns and making the little bend in the road. Aaron noticed numbers on all the mailboxes.

Then they were there. The house, large and silent-looking, had not changed. Of this Aaron was glad. The shake roof, the large stone fireplace between two windows, the spot where there had always been flowers that now had begonias still blooming in oranges, yellows, and reds. And then he caught a glimpse of the bay. The water, a clear, deep blue, seemed to go on forever. It was calm—no whitecaps today. Aaron couldn't wait to get the binoculars to see more.

"Dad!" He bounded out of the car, leaving his duffel in the trunk. He could get that later. "I can walk on the mud flats."

"Better get boots."

"Are they in the furnace room?"

"Same place."

Running into the garage, Aaron opened the door where they'd kept boots and extra coats and hats. A twenty-five-pound bag of birdseed stood on the floor. This must be Alice's hobby, he decided.

He pulled the boots on over his stocking feet and grabbed a hat, just in case the wind came up.

"I'm off!"

Aaron ran down the narrow road where his father drove the old truck, past the shed where he'd kept tools at one time, and crossed over onto one of the trails. There was the garden spot. Cornstalks stood and swayed in the breeze. Dad and his garden. He always had to have a garden. Aaron had liked everything but the zucchini.

He thought of Deanna again and the night she served sautéed sliced zucchini wedges. He'd eaten them and decided they weren't as bad as he recalled from when he was younger. No way would he not eat what she fixed.

When the tide was out, there were acres of mud flats. One could go clamming here, could dig for the small clams people loved. He would not do that. He just wanted to walk along and smell the clean air, feel the breeze on his face, and go back in time—to when he often walked here with Hannah tagging along. Aaron found a log and sat, looking out at the wide expanse of the Willapa Bay. Some things never change, he decided, and for that he was grateful. Some things do change, though, and that was what he needed to get used to.

It was an hour before Aaron headed back to the house. The smell of coffee filled the air as he slipped out of the boots and left them in the furnace room. He walked down the long hall toward the kitchen and living area.

A new floor had been laid. It looked nice. He stopped at the entrance of the small bedroom, the one that had been Hannah's. There used to be a blue carpet on the floor, as Hannah loved blue. Her small bed had butted up against one wall, and a dresser had stood against another. They were gone now, and the thought of his little sister coughing, getting sicker and sicker in this room, made him want to bang the wall. How could this be an office now? That meant every memory of Hannah was gone. He didn't even see a photo of her. How could his father just forget her like that? He wondered now, something he hadn't thought about until this minute: Where was his sister buried? Was it in the old Oysterville Cemetery, a place so close that he could go and visit her grave? He'd have to ask.

A computer sat on his grandfather's old desk.

Aaron went in and looked at the photos of his family members: Grandpa and Grandma Walker, his mother's family, and cousins. These used to be in the hall. There was even a small photo of his mother on the wall by a photo of Hannah. The knot in his throat grew tight.

"Aaron? I thought I heard you come in." His father was there, slipping an arm around his shoulder. "Does it seem much different?"

"The bay, no; the outside of the house and the yard, no. I see you've cut down trees and cleared out some of the brush."

Leighton nodded. "Just to give us a better view." His father cleared his voice. "How about the house?"

"This was Hannah's room, and you took everything out."

"I saved it all. I moved it down to Luke's old bedroom."

"But why?"

Leighton's eyes filled with sudden tears. "I couldn't walk by every day and see her bed, the posters on the wall, and not think of her. It seemed better this way."

Aaron nodded, knowing he would have felt the same had he been here.

"Dad, what happened to Cora?"

His father's face looked blank for a long moment. "Cora has gone to Oregon. She's working for a hazelnut farmer there."

"Cora's left the peninsula? I find that hard to believe."

"Sometimes change is good for a person."

Aaron leaned over and looked at another row of photos, ones he didn't recognize.

"This is some of Alice's family. Her sister, daughter, son-in-law, and the baby, of course."

And then he saw the wedding picture, his father and Alice coming out of the Oysterville Church while people waved and threw rice at them. Only it wasn't rice anymore, but birdseed. It was the ecological thing to do.

"I can see you and Alice are happy," Aaron said.

"I didn't think it would ever happen to me," Leighton answered. "I never considered remarrying. When you botch up one marriage, you just think it's better not to try again."

Aaron leaned over the computer. "Dad, I'd like to send a quick message to my friend."

"Sure. And when you're finished, come and have some coffee while Alice finishes dinner. I think we're having clam fritters tonight."

"I should have brought you lobster. . . ."

"Lobsters would be nice, but that's okay," Leighton said. "You go ahead and send your mail, then we'll talk."

Aaron brought up the E-mail and typed in Deanna's address. He put that on hold and went back to the Internet, typing in Courtney's address, which he'd used to contact Deanna the previous night. There was a message:

Aaron,
Dad has not been well, but I think it's just the flu. He wouldn't go get a flu shot, though they offered them at

*the grange hall. He's stubborn, as you well know. I think
a lot of men are that way.*

   *Maddy asks every day when you are going to come to
see us. I made the mistake of saying you might come back
one day, not to live here, but to visit. She picked up on that
and won't let the subject drop. Murph is still looking for
you too. When we walk down the trail past the cottage, he
stops and whines at the door, as if you were there and will
suddenly appear and throw the Frisbee.*

Aaron reread the letter, looking for some sign that Deanna
might miss him too, but it wasn't there. The old man, the kid,
and the dog missed him. He guessed that would just have to do.

He went back to his letter and told her this would be his
regular address now. The other had just been for one night.

Deanna,

   *Hello. See if you can get GB to talk your father into
seeing a doctor. He might listen to him.*

   *In some ways everything seems to have changed here,
but in other ways, it is the same. The bay is calm and
peaceful, and I walked along the mud flats. It's different
here than at Penabscot Bay. I wish you could see it
sometime.*

   *I can't get used to the idea of my father remarrying,
but Alice seems okay, and she loves him. I can certainly
see that.*

   *It's almost dinnertime. I hope to hear from you.
Please give Maddy a big hug for me and throw the
Frisbee a couple of times for Murph. Tell Mick I hope he
feels better soon.*

                                        *Your friend,
                                         Aaron Walker*

Aaron reread his letter, visualizing Deanna sitting at the desk. It was almost as if she were in the room with him. He shut down the computer and went down the hall.

The table was set with new blue chinaware that Aaron had never seen. It had to be Alice's. There was French bread on the table already and bowls for salad.

There were several additions to the house—the new dishes, pictures and paintings on the walls, and a new easy chair—but the dining-room table and chairs were the same as he remembered, as were the love seat and couch in the living room. A baby grand piano with a glossy black finish sat in one corner. Hannah had been the only one who played it. He remembered her fingers running up and down the keyboard. "Such grace," the piano teacher said. "She has a natural talent for it, Mr. Walker."

"Then she will continue with lessons," Leighton had said. "She needs something to feel good about, and I can't think of a better thing than music."

Alice brought clam fritters and baked potatoes to the table. "This is it. Guess we can eat now."

After his father blessed the meal, Alice began passing the food.

"What are your plans, Aaron?" his father asked once the meal was over and they had taken coffee into the living room.

"I want to get my own crabbing boat."

"You have money for a boat?"

Aaron's cheeks flushed. "Well, not exactly."

"You've used your inheritance?"

"Yeah, Dad, guess I did. It costs money to travel, to pay for a place to stay, food—you know, the usual expenses."

"Yes, I do know."

"I suppose I should have saved that money for the boat. I shouldn't have left at all. I know that's what you are thinking."

"I didn't say that, Aaron."

"But you're thinking it." He expected his Dad's jaw to tighten as it had in the old days. The steam would come rolling out his ears any moment now. But he got up from the table and sat on the old familiar love seat in front of the window, looking out at the bay and saying nothing.

"I had to go at the time."

"I figured that out."

"You didn't seem to want me here."

"What?" The voice rose just a bit.

"You told me to get out that last night. . . ."

"Is that what this is about? I told you to get out, yes, but I meant out of the room, for Pete's sake."

"I know, but I needed you too, Dad, and there just wasn't enough of you to go around."

His father kept staring out the window. Alice took his hand in hers, then leaned over to kiss his cheek. "Your father has worried about you endlessly."

"Yeah, right."

"Aaron! You must show respect for Alice."

"I'm sorry," Aaron said, looking at her briefly.

"I don't want to talk about this now," his father said. "I think we need to wait, think over things, and discuss it at a later time."

"You mean sweep things under the rug like we always used to do?"

"No. I want to discuss it, but only when we are both calm and even-tempered."

"Whatever. Do I still have the same bedroom downstairs?"

"Of course. If that's what you want."

Aaron clumped down the stairs, refusing Alice's offer of apple pie à la mode. He couldn't stick around. No way. It had gone as he predicted, except that his father had not blown his top like he had expected. He seemed calmer and definitely more at ease.

The bedroom was unchanged. As Aaron looked around at the same curtains at the windows, blue with sailboats, the light-blue walls, and the four-poster bed with the fish design bedspread, a lump came to his throat. How could nothing have changed? It was as if he'd never left. Hadn't anyone slept here? Well, he supposed not, since his brothers were older and lived elsewhere.

Aaron looked at his old baseball mitt and ball. The team had signed the baseball after his home run in the playoffs. He held the mitt and lightly tossed the ball into it. That seemed so terribly long ago now.

Footsteps sounded overhead as he lay across the bed. He was tired—his inner clock was still three hours ahead. He supposed he should go and apologize. He should have thanked his father for sending the money, should have told him how good it was to be home, should have at least said, "I love you, Dad," but "I love you" had not come from his father's mouth either. He thought of what was said at the airport.

"It's good to have you back, Son."

"I missed you, Dad."

"You're looking good, a bit taller."

It was superficial, not what Aaron had needed to hear. Not "I love you, Aaron." Perhaps those words would never be said. He was probably wishing for something that could not happen.

He remembered his duffel bag and went out the basement door and up the steps that led to the side yard. The duffel bag was out of the trunk and standing at the top of the steps going down. It was as if his father knew he would come this way and find his belongings.

Aaron slung it over his shoulder and headed back down and

to the basement. He'd freshen up a bit, then go back upstairs and attempt an apology. Would his father accept it? At this point he didn't know. He couldn't be sure of anything. Too many changes, and he hadn't been here for any of them.

seventeen

The living room was dark, and Aaron thought his father and Alice had gone to bed. The conversation could wait until another time. He wasn't sure how his father would react when he said "thank you" and "I love you."

"Aaron?"

He jumped. "Dad? You sitting in the dark?"

"Yes. I enjoy watching the lights across the bay; gives me a sense of peace, of fulfillment somehow. Come sit beside me."

"Alice?"

"She's in the bedroom, reading. That's one of her favorite pastimes, and far be it from me to try to change her habits after this many years."

"Dad?"

"Yes?"

He saw the outline of his father's jaw, could reach out and touch him, if he chose. He looked straight ahead, knowing it was more difficult to look at someone when you confronted them or offered thanks. He didn't want to get sidetracked now.

"How do you know when you are in love?"

The question surprised even him. It wasn't what he meant to say at all. How could he have asked it?

A low chuckle sounded from his father. "Somehow, I didn't think that would be the topic of conversation."

"Neither did I!"

"You did meet someone. The person you e-mailed earlier."

"I like her a lot, Dad. She's a beautiful, Christian young woman, raising a child by herself. Her husband was lost at sea. One of those quick storms that come up."

"Oh, I'm sorry to hear that."

"She writes how everyone misses me—not that I've been gone that long—but she doesn't say a word about her—you know, if she misses me."

"It's too painful, I suspect."

"Why? What do you mean?"

"Have you told her how you feel?"

"No."

"Then that's what I mean."

"She knows. I'm sure she knows."

"Not if you don't say the words. Women have to hear the words. I made that mistake with your mother; I should have told her every day that I loved her. It might have made a difference."

"Do you tell Alice?"

"I sure do."

"Sure do what?"

Neither had heard the feet cross the floor.

"I heard voices," she said. "I thought you were watching TV."

"In the dark?"

"I walk around in the dark." She sat in the rocker and rose as quickly as she'd sat. "I think you two were talking. Sorry I interrupted."

"It's okay."

"No. It's not," Alice said. "Good night, Aaron."

After she'd left, Leighton told Aaron about their courtship. "I knew the first time I saw her that she was going to become something special in my life. She had this laugh that was contagious, and I just liked her manner. But I had a problem convincing her at first. In fact, I gave up at one point but then went back to her house. I was on my way back home here when I realized I had to try once more. I had to make her see how I really felt."

"And she accepted it."

"No, not exactly."

"Not exactly? What do you mean?"

"She had a life that was full—her daughter, the expected baby, a sister, her part-time job, her volunteer work. She didn't need a man in her life."

"Oh."

"Yeah, that's hard to take when you want to become part of someone's life."

"Well, something must have happened to change her mind."

"I think God did it. Heaven knows I said enough prayers."

"It isn't ever easy, I take it."

Leighton laughed. "You're young, Aaron. You have your whole life ahead of you."

"But if you know—"

"If you know, you need to step forward and make something happen. It won't happen on its own."

Aaron thought of the apology he'd meant to convey, but somehow he couldn't say it now. Why couldn't he say a simple "I love you" to his own father? If he couldn't do that, how did he think he ever could speak those words to Deanna or any other woman who came into his life?

&

Deanna knew the cottage would be empty. Empty of Aaron's belongings. But it seemed his presence was here. He'd made the bed, swept the floors, and the curtains were still tied back. He liked it that way, so he could see outside better.

The hurt crept up her toes, through her midsection, and on to her heart. How was she going to forget him and go on with her life?

She looked under the bed, hoping there'd be a sock or a pair of shoes—something he'd left behind. There was nothing. She smelled the bedspread to see if his scent was left behind. He never wore cologne, so she didn't expect to smell anything, and yet there was a certain scent as she lay across the bed and let the tears come.

Deanna didn't know how long she'd been here at the cottage when she suddenly thought of Maddy. She'd left her coloring in the living room. How long had she been gone? Her father was there, but she wasn't certain he'd think before going outside and leaving his granddaughter alone.

She sprang from the bed, took one last look at the cottage, then headed down the path. Murphy was waiting and whined.

"I know. You miss him too." She bent down and ruffled the dog's fur. "But he'll be back. I must believe that, Murph."

Deanna hurried back up the path to the house.

Maddy was still coloring, but looked up and smiled. "Mommy! I was looking all over for you!"

Deanna leaned over and pulled her child close. "Honey, I shouldn't have left you alone. Are you okay?"

"I drew a picture for Aaron."

The hurt stabbed at her again. "It's beautiful, and in blues and reds, his favorite colors."

"When can I give it to him?" She looked up out of serious eyes, waiting.

"Honey, Aaron had to leave unexpectedly, but you know what?" And suddenly her heart lifted. "We'll e-mail it to him. We can send it as an attachment! I'm so glad we bought that scanner."

The door opened, and Mick came in. "It's kind of lonely around here, isn't it?"

"Yes, Dad, it is."

"He won't be back, you know."

Deanna felt the ache start again, deep within her. "No, I suppose not."

Her father looked at her for a long moment. "There'll be someone else, Daughter."

"But Aaron's coming back because he loves me," Maddy said then.

Deanna wished she could say the same. If only she could bank on that fact.

"That boy has a lot of thinking to do," her father said. "He'll straighten things out with his family. Then, if he is ready, and I repeat, if, he might come back, and you will have your answer."

Deanna chewed her lower lip.

Mick strode over and poured a mug of coffee. "I've said my piece, and I won't say another word about it."

Deanna leaned over and hugged the back of her father's shoulder. "I know, Daddy." She rarely called him Daddy anymore, and he turned and held her tight for a brief moment.

Maddy had folded the colored picture and handed it to her mother. "It's for when you find Aaron."

And that night he had sent a message, and hope soared once again. Not that he said he missed her, but he let her know that he'd arrived okay, and if she was reading right between the lines, he missed all of them. It was a hope she had to hold close. Just maybe God had heard her prayers after all.

eighteen

The first morning after returning to Oysterville, Aaron rose early, before his father or Alice. It seemed funny to get up before it was light out, but it wasn't four in the morning to him—his inner clock said it was seven.

He donned rubber boots, a hat, and a heavy jacket from the furnace room. It would be cold this early on the bay. It would be cold anywhere on the peninsula. It was the third week in November.

Soon his nose and eyelashes were covered with a light mist that was falling as he made his way down the path to the bay. He'd grabbed a couple of cookies from the cookie jar in the kitchen and took one out of his pocket. Peanut butter, one of his favorites.

He had something else in his pocket. He'd found it in a dresser drawer last night. Grandpa's old harmonica. Aaron played a few bars of "Amazing Grace." Music soothed him, as it had Hannah. Sometimes they played together, and "Amazing Grace" had been her favorite hymn. He wondered now if it had been played at her funeral. The knot returned to his throat.

He had been a coward. It was true. He should have stayed and spent what time he could with her. Had she missed him? He couldn't ask his father or his brothers. Nobody would know. Aaron thought of asking God for a sign. Was that wrong? He needed to know that Hannah had forgiven him, that, yes, she had missed him, but had understood why he couldn't stay.

He sat on an old log at his favorite spot and waited for the dawn to slip up over the Willapa Hills. It was an awesome sight on a clear morning. The mist had stopped, but he felt the spray from the bay as a gentle breeze rolled across the water. A crabbing boat, with lights on, went north, and he waved. He was certain the skipper couldn't see him, but he didn't care. He felt better about waving. Should he talk his father into helping him buy a boat? It might be two or three years before he could pay for it. Was it what he really wanted now?

The tide was going out, and soon he could walk on the mud flats again. They weren't pretty, but there was food in the mud. The sandpipers flew over from the beach side, a mile or so away, looking for shrimp barely discernible with the naked eye.

He played another tune, one his father used to whistle a lot, "There's Something about That Name." Aaron couldn't remember the words, but the tune stuck with him: "Yes, there was something about the name of Jesus."

Aaron played yet another tune that he hadn't thought of in a long while, "She'll be Coming around the Mountain." He'd heard Deanna humming it more than once, usually while the bacon or ham sizzled. It was probably because she was in a good mood or as she had said one morning, "I feel especially blessed today."

The choked feeling returned as he put the harmonica away. How could he make a new life when his thoughts constantly returned to the house on the hill and the woman in the kitchen, bustling around each morning feeding her father and daughter, and then later adding Aaron to the family around the table. She never complained and took things in her stride. He thought of Mick, who had treated him like a son, had trusted that Aaron would be good for the rent on the cottage. And GB. He didn't miss him, but he wondered if anyone really missed GB.

Another crabber went north. Aaron didn't bother to wave.

The light was seeping through the trees now, and soon the sun would appear, adding its pinkish-red glow to the horizon. It was a sight he would never grow tired of. Yet there were gorgeous sunrises and sunsets on the East Coast as well, and there was someone to share them with there. He thought of the night they had nearly collided on the path, the day they picked blueberries, the picnic lunch at the park on a blanket, with Maddy between them. Her hand felt soft in his callused one, and it hit him then that he could go on all through the rest of his life with this woman. Yet he had left, returning to the area of his birth.

"Hello. Am I intruding?"

Aaron almost fell off the log as he whirled to find Alice bundled in a long jacket with a blue stocking cap covering her head.

"I—that is—I like to come sit here."

"I bet you've missed it."

He swallowed hard. "Yes, I have. Do you always get up this early?"

"Usually not, but my heart has been troubled lately."

"It has?" He moved over so there was enough room on the log for Alice to sit. She sat beside him and looked out over the bay, clasping her hands in front of her.

"Aaron, I love your father with all my heart."

"Yes, I know. I can tell."

"Are you okay with the idea that he found someone after all these years?"

Aaron turned and stared at the small woman beside him. She made him think of Deanna, except the hair wasn't right. And there were lines around her eyes and wrinkles here and there. "I am fine with it, and anyone can tell he loves you."

Alice hugged her knees close. "You really think so?"

"Yeah, I do."

There was a moment of silence, and then Alice spoke. "I

didn't come to discuss your father or me. I want to know about you, Aaron. You're a true enigma if ever I saw one."

"I am?" He would never have classified himself in that way.

"Yes, you are. What's going on in that head of yours, I find myself wondering."

Aaron didn't want to discuss it, and especially not with someone he hardly knew. Yet she sat silently, as if waiting for him to say something, so he guessed he'd have to try to explain.

"You know about Hannah. . . ."

"Oh, yes. And I know how it tore your father apart because he couldn't do anything. I understand that so completely. I never was able to have children, and when my Courtney came down with a mysterious ailment when she was fifteen, I was grief-stricken, so fearful she would be taken away from me."

"Courtney is adopted?

"Yes."

"I didn't know that."

"But back to Hannah. I am thinking you left because you and she were close, and you couldn't do anything to help her. . . ."

Tears pressed against his eyelids. "She coughed so much more; she couldn't go out to play, could no longer go to school. It was awful. And the last night I was home, my father— well, he didn't understand why I wanted to be with her. He asked me to leave and not come back."

"Oh, Aaron, he didn't mean never come back."

"I know that now."

She put an arm around him. "So you ran because it was the only thing you could think of to do."

"Something like that."

"But to never call, never write—that's what I don't understand. Your father not only lost his beloved Hannah, he lost you as well."

Aaron felt the old hurt return as he dug his boot into the

soft ground. Oh, he had words to say, words to defend himself, but nobody would understand, and especially not Alice or his father.

"You think he didn't love you because he didn't give you any time."

"He worked and worked, and Cora pretty much helped us out. And before that an aunt stayed with us." *All I ever wanted was for him to say he loved me, to put an arm around me. Was that expecting too much?* is what Aaron wanted to say.

"Do you suppose you two could make up? I mean, really make up. God teaches us to forgive. Not that we can completely forget, but we need to learn the lesson of forgiveness."

"I don't think he's forgiven me."

"Oh, I think he has. I know he has."

Alice stood. "This is one of the most beautiful spots I've ever seen, and to think I would never have seen it if it hadn't been for your father's laptop."

Aaron nodded. "I have always loved the bay. I like the ocean too, but it isn't serene like this."

"Let's go have breakfast. Those cookies you took earlier couldn't have filled the hole much."

"You knew?"

"I heard the jar lid scrape just as I was getting up."

Aaron laughed. It had made a certain sound, but he'd never worried before about sneaking food out.

"I'm going over to see an old friend—thought I'd have breakfast there."

"Looking like that?"

Aaron shrugged. "Why not? I just look like an oysterman. It's pretty common around here."

"Do you want to use my car?"

He smiled. "Yeah, sure."

❧

Jill was pouring coffee when he entered the small café. She

glanced up, her eyes widening in surprise. "Aaron Walker! Is it really you?"

He went over and gave her a brief hug. "Yep, one and the same."

"When did you get into town?"

"Two nights ago."

He watched while she made the rounds, then brought a customer's order. Finally, she came with order pad in hand. She looked the same, and it surprised him. He didn't know why, but he thought she would have aged. Her hair was long and blond, pulled back into a ponytail. He remembered asking her once if she would get married in a ponytail, and her answer had been, "Yes, and is that a proposal, Aaron?"

She had a trim figure, and her eyes were the same brown with hazel flecks. He had always liked her eyes.

"So? Are you back for good?"

"Yeah, I think so."

"Where were you all those years?"

"Here and there. Mostly in Maine, though."

"Maine! That's thousands of miles away."

"Yeah, I know. I liked it, though. Quiet. Sort of made me think of Oysterville."

"Are you wanting to go out or something? We could take in a movie down in Long Beach."

Aaron remembered the movie house. He and Jill used to go a lot when they were dating. It was either that or bowling.

The door opened, and he recognized both guys sauntering in. They'd all gone to the same high school, the only one on the peninsula. He waved, and then they were talking, asking him the same questions Jill had. He supposed it would always be like this. In a small town, people either didn't move away, or, if they did, they didn't come back. He had done both, so that made him unusual. Maybe that was what Alice meant when she said he was an enigma.

"Hey, let's go have a few beers tonight, shoot some pool at Doc's."

"It's still here?"

"Right on the same corner, Man."

Aaron didn't want to say that he didn't drink anymore. He had at the logging camp, but it was too easy to let it take over your life. And he knew it didn't glorify God. Now that he was searching for answers, it wasn't right to let drinking be part of his life.

"Thanks, guys, but Jill and I are going to a movie."

"You and Jill, just like before, huh?"

"Yes, just like before." Jill brought his toast. "Are you sure this is all you want?

"This is fine." He didn't want to say he was hoarding his last bit of wages and wondered if he even wanted to spend money for movie tickets. He could hit his father up eventually or maybe ask Alice. She seemed more approachable.

"Just coffee," the guys said.

Aaron stayed long enough to say hello to another group of people he remembered from school days. One was a retired teacher, the other, the librarian.

"Are we going to the late movie?" Jill asked as she refilled his cup.

"Sure. What time? And you'll have to tell me where you live now."

She laughed. "Oh, I'm back home again, Aaron. Living with my mom. I was divorced a year ago and just didn't have the money for an apartment."

"Divorced?" He pretended he hadn't heard it already.

"Yes."

"Someone I know?"

"Maybe. He worked for your father once. We started dating after you left. He's gone now, though." She laughed again as she tossed her head. "No children, so I'm lucky there."

Aaron pushed his chair back. Married. Divorced. No kids. Jill thought that was the way it was supposed to be, because her mother had been divorced three times.

"Say, do you still like that crazy musical, *Fiddler on the Roof*?"

It was Aaron's turn to laugh now. He had the tape in the car, the car he'd left behind in East Belfast. He hadn't remembered about it until now.

"Yeah, I still like that musical."

"I always liked hearing you sing along with it. You have a good voice, you know."

Aaron thanked Jill for the compliment, finished his breakfast, and waved as he pulled out of the parking lot. He wondered if he should borrow his father's truck for tonight.

He drove through town and noticed Jack's Country Store. It was an icon in the area—had been there since he could remember. He went by the library and stopped at a resort where he had worked one summer mowing the lawn and keeping the grounds up. He had decided then he would never be a gardener. No, he was a fisherman, a man who loved the water.

His mind went to Deanna again. She was different than Jill. Though they hadn't gone out yet, he knew after a brief conversation that Jill was flighty, had no real goals. He almost wanted to back out of the date.

Mist began falling as he drove east then north, heading for Oysterville and home.

Home. It sounded funny, not quite right. Would he feel at home again soon?

nineteen

Alice was in the kitchen making cookies. "Can't seem to keep the cookie jar full."

"Thanks for use of the car."

"Anytime." Alice glanced up. "Why don't you take it tonight and go find some friends?"

"You were reading my mind," Aaron said. "Actually, I visited an old friend, and she suggested a movie tonight."

"That should be fun."

"What should be fun?" Leighton asked as he padded into the kitchen looking from his wife to his son. "Been busy answering orders for oysters. Some from as far away as New York."

Aaron couldn't get over the fact that his father was retired now. It seemed strange not to have him leave for work in the morning. He also never dreamed his father would buy a computer, much less use it.

"Dad! I have an idea. I'd like to send some oysters to Mick and his family."

"The place where you last worked?"

"Yes. They'd enjoy getting oysters. And maybe they could send us a lobster. How about that?"

"Oh, I love lobster," Alice said. "I've read about the lobster pounds on the East Coast."

"Maybe you could go out and see firsthand," Aaron said. "That would be a good trip for you two to take. By the way, can I use the computer?"

"Sure," Leighton answered. "I'm going over to the store. Why don't you come, Aaron? I can wait a few minutes."

"I'll just walk down there."

"It's two miles."

"I can handle it."

Leighton leaned over and kissed Alice. "I'll be back in time for lunch. I wouldn't miss your clam chowder for anything."

Aaron found, not one, but two letters from Deanna.

"Maddy says hello," the first one began. *"She's drawn you two pictures now. We all miss you."*

All? It was the first time she'd included herself in the "missed you" part. A warm feeling filled him.

The second message made him sit up.

"Dad's still not doing well. Not sure what it is. If I didn't know better, I'd say he was having heart problems, but he says, 'My ol' ticker is working just fine, thank you very much.'"

What could it be? Aaron stared at the screen, but instead of the words, he was seeing a crusty old man, as stubborn as they come, chewing on the end of his cherry-wood pipe.

He hit the Respond button.

"Do you need for me to come help?" Aaron wanted to ask. He wanted to, but how could he disappoint his father about Thanksgiving? His brothers, their wives, and the assorted grandchildren were coming, along with Alice's family, and he must be here for that. It was a combination "welcome home" and Thanksgiving meal.

"I'm going down to the Sea Gift Farms with my dad," Aaron typed out. *"A surprise is coming your way. Your father will love it! I pray for his quick recovery."*

Later, he wondered why he hadn't told her how much he missed her, how he couldn't get her smiling face out of his mind. . . .

ঞ

The store was different from what Aaron remembered, and he stared in amazement. The large room where workers sorted oysters had not changed, but there was an addition—a gift store. Canned salmon, sturgeon, and oysters filled the shelves. Various cookbooks lined up on a bottom shelf, and spices were on the counter in special gift baskets. Friday's bread had been baked and had sold out within an hour of coming in.

"Dad, this is looking good."

"How about working here, Aaron? You could manage the store—I've got one gal moving to Seattle, and my other helper is going back to school after Christmas. What do you think?"

Aaron hesitated. He had told his father that he wanted to be a crabber, that being on the water was important, was what he'd dreamed about since he was ten or so.

"Sleep on it," Leighton said. "Thought you could do this for awhile until you get your crabbing boat."

Aaron met his father's steady gaze. He had remembered after all. "Yeah, Dad, you're right."

After shipping off a package of smoked oysters to Maine—he'd decided on smoked oysters because they didn't require dry ice—he wished he'd be there when the package arrived.

"Let's go have some of Alice's great clam chowder," Leighton said.

He rode back with his father, knowing it was time to ask about Hannah, though he felt awkward about bringing it up.

"Dad, where is Hannah buried?"

His father swallowed, staring straight ahead. "In the Lone Fir Cemetery, next to her maternal grandparents. It's off of Sandridge Road."

"Yeah, I remember. I want to go there."

"Yes, I think you need to see it." Leighton finally looked over at his son. "Perhaps tomorrow would be a good time for us to go."

❧

It was early when Aaron left for his date. He wore khakis and a navy blue wool sweater. He had an errand to run first, before darkness fell.

He drove down Sandridge, the "back road" as the old-timers

called it. He stopped at Clarke's Nursery, buying a bronze chrysanthemum for Alice. It would look nice in the center of the Thanksgiving table. He also bought a small bouquet of carnations. Pink. Hannah had liked pink.

It was dusk by the time he reached the winding road to Lone Fir Cemetery. Maybe he should have waited for his father, but this was something he needed to do alone. Aaron felt a growing tightness as he drove up the small incline toward the spot. He remembered going here when an aunt died. Remembered the cold, rainy morning, standing beside his father while Hannah stood on the other side. It had been a short service with a song sung, Scripture read, and the words of the pastor. They'd left immediately, as his father was worried about Hannah catching cold, as colds laid her up for days.

It wasn't cold today. It wasn't warm either, just a typical gray November day, but unusually calm. He stopped at the top of the U-shaped drive and got out. He knew exactly where the family plot was and sauntered past a few other graves; all the while the tightness grew.

Then he saw it, and he gripped the carnation stems. He hadn't thought it would be this difficult. The gray marble slab looked newer than most. Aaron bent down and read the inscription:

OUR ANGEL

HANNAH ELIZABETH WALKER

BORN APRIL 15, 1984

DEPARTED OCTOBER 20, 1999

SHE WILL LIVE IN OUR HEARTS FOREVER

Aaron traced the letters of her name. Bending the carnation stems, he made a heart and laid them on the grave. Sorrow welled up inside. How could this be? She was too young to die.

"I loved you more than anything, Hannah, but I know your spirit is up in heaven with Jesus. This is for you, Hannah." He took out the harmonica and began playing "Amazing Grace." He played several verses, pausing more than once to wipe away the tears, then knelt down again. "I'm so sorry I wasn't there for you." He closed his eyes. "God, please forgive me, and take away this guilt. Draw me close, let me know and depend on You as Deanna does."

Aaron knew he wouldn't be back, but it didn't matter anymore. He felt cleansed. Free from sin and guilt. He would always have Hannah in his heart. Nothing would ever change that. Aaron got to his feet, thanking God for the peaceful, calm moment, as there wasn't even a breeze. As if in answer, a ripple of wind touched his face, then was gone. He smiled, knowing it was a sign of God's presence.

He walked back to the car, feeling lighter than he had in a very long time.

Aaron didn't want to keep the date with Jill, but he didn't want to call her to tell her he wasn't coming either. Nor was he ready to go back to Oysterville. Perhaps the movie would be a good diversion.

He drove by the docks in Ilwaco, looking out over the boats in the slips. It was past fishing season, so the boats were idle. Two men drank coffee on the stern of one. He waved in passing. A new restaurant had opened, a coffee shop, plus a trendy little gift shop. There was a pizza parlor, but it had a FOR SALE sign in the window. That was too bad, as it would have been nice to pick up something after the movie. It also would have been nice to look out over the water as they sipped colas and ate pizza.

After leaving the docks, Aaron drove through town and up the hill past the old grade school, although it was now a middle school, then down the road past the high school. The mascot, a fisherman in a bright yellow raincoat, stood in front with a dilapidated old boat at the school's entrance. Everything looked the same. The concrete steps leading up to the school, the football field with its covered bleachers. Aaron swallowed hard, remembering how he'd gone out for football and hated it. The next fall he ran cross-country, and that was more to his liking. In the summer he played baseball. But mostly, he didn't care about school sports. He just liked to be on the water.

It was almost seven, so he drove back up the hill and toward the house where Jill lived. He wondered what Deanna was doing now and if Mick felt better today. Why couldn't he get the little family out of his mind? He knew Deanna, and soon she'd write a letter and include Maddy's drawings. She just did things like that.

The front door opened, and Jill's mother motioned him to come in.

"Goodness, it's been a long time, Aaron, but you haven't changed a bit." She smiled and touched his arm. "I think you have more muscles."

"It's from working," he said. "I was at a logging camp for a year. Now that's hard labor."

"What's hard labor?" Jill asked as she entered the room. She wore a short, tight skirt, and her hair was down around her face. He could never remember seeing her look like this. She walked up and hugged him. "You're looking good," she said.

He swallowed hard, knowing her statement required a response from him. "And you too."

"You guys have fun. Catch up on the good ol' times," Mrs. Benson called with a wave.

"We do have time to slip into the Anchor Tavern for a quick beer."

"I don't drink beer," he answered.

"Don't drink beer?" She looked at him as if she couldn't believe what she'd just heard. "But everyone drinks beer."

"I'd like to stop for an ice cream cone. I noticed a new little store close to the gas station."

"Oh. Well, okay."

Aaron knew the evening would not go well. He hoped the movie was worth seeing. He also hoped that nothing was expected of him later. Not that Jill wasn't nice, and not that they didn't have a history together, but right now he was wondering why he'd agreed to a date. He didn't feel he belonged here, not anymore.

"We can walk on the beach or stroll the boardwalk," Jill suggested. "We don't have to see the movie. It's up to you."

"No, it's a comedy. Should be fun. We can walk later."

Aaron managed to make it through the evening. He laughed at the movie. He and Jill shared a big tub of popcorn, but when their hands touched, he felt nothing. Jill seemed more like a cousin or an old friend, not a girlfriend.

"You're preoccupied," she said when they got into the car. They stopped at the only place open and had a cup of coffee, though she suggested a tavern again.

"You've changed," she continued. "You're not like the Aaron I remember."

"I know."

"I suppose you want to take me home."

"Yes, I think so. Jill, I'm sorry. I just can't see picking up where we left off."

"There's someone else?" She leaned over and pulled his face down. "I don't want to see you leave a second time. You'll adjust. It just takes time."

"Jill, what we had once was good, but we were just kids then. I've grown in a different direction and so have you."

"It's because I suggested having a beer. . . ."

"No, it isn't that. It's just not going to work out. You and me."

After he walked her up the sidewalk, her mother opened the door and looked out. Of course she'd been watching from the window and had undoubtedly expected Aaron to either come in or to at least kiss Jill on the porch, but he'd hugged her briefly instead.

"Kinda early," she said as Jill rushed past.

Aaron drove home, his head whirling with thoughts. Maybe he didn't belong here. All he thought of was Deanna, the way she made him feel. He wondered if she would still be up when he got back to Oysterville. He doubted it, but he'd send an E-mail anyway.

❧

Later, Aaron sat in the office, thinking about Hannah again. He opened the bottom drawer, where he'd found his harmonica earlier. This must be the drawer his father referred to, the one where Hannah had kept her treasures. Under a stack of children's books, he found the small, leather-bound book with DIARY printed across the front in gold. Was this Hannah's? He'd never seen her writing in anything but the spiral notebook, where she jotted down poems. Where was it? He'd love to read some of her work now. Hannah's poems often rhymed, but not always. Aaron had memorized one:

IF I HAD ONE WISH

I wish I could run and play
   I wish I wouldn't cough
And if wishes were roses
   We'd all smell good.

He found a small box with stickers, barrettes, and a sand dollar they'd found on the beach one day. They often found broken ones, but this was a perfect, whole one, and Hannah had held it high. "For my collection," she'd said.

Aaron touched the diary, wanting to open it, wanting to read, but not daring to, as it was personal. Still, who would know? He opened the pages, flipping through until he came to the year and month he had left. His name leaped off the page.

"Aaron left last night. I thought he might some day. He's so worried about me, but I wish he wouldn't be. I don't blame him for going, though I'll miss him something fierce. But I know he will be happy wherever he goes. Aaron has a way of making people smile."

He gripped the small book, a lump coming to his throat at the memory. And now he knew she loved him, that she had forgiven him for leaving like that; she had even expected it. Yet why hadn't he been strong for her? Why, he was no better than her mother, who couldn't handle her child's illness.

The light came on, and his father stood in the doorway. "Aaron? I got up thinking I heard a noise. Is something wrong?"

Aaron lurched to his feet, the words pouring out. "Dad, I went to the cemetery earlier. I left flowers on Hannah's grave. It was wrong of me to leave when she needed me. Can you ever forgive me? Will you love me again like you used to when I was little and we'd take those trips to Portland?"

"What?" Leighton grabbed his son tight to his chest. "Aaron, I never stopped loving you, though it may have seemed like it. And as for forgiving, how could I not forgive you when God has taught us that forgiveness is one of the most important of all things?"

As the hurt of the past five years poured out, each spoke of things that had hurt, things they had not understood, and Aaron knew he was forgiven, and it was just like Alice said. He also knew that if he left again, it would be under different circumstances and for different reasons. Good reasons this time. He felt led to return to Maine, and Leighton would understand. This time he'd have his father's approval. But he couldn't tell him until after Thanksgiving.

twenty

Preparations were made for the Thanksgiving feast. Alice baked both a ham and a turkey.

"Why both?" Aaron asked.

"Because we have eighteen people coming."

"Eighteen?" Aaron had counted sixteen.

"Well, we can't leave out dear Mrs. Endicott and her sister. They are all alone, and since neither likes to cook, I had to ask them."

Leighton nodded. "Definitely. Alice always thinks of things like that."

Aaron remembered the Endicott family that lived in Oysterville, but they had never been invited to dinner, let alone a Thanksgiving meal.

"I also asked my sister, Agnes, but she hates riding in a car this far, so I guess she will never see the beautiful peninsula or Willapa Bay."

Aaron wasn't sure when it hit him, but probably after everyone had arrived. Coats and hats were hung in both hall closets, Luke's kids were involved in playing a game of Risk on the card table, and the men watched the football game while they waited for John to arrive from Portland. Aaron looked around, and in that house full of people, teeming with noise and loud greetings, he felt alone, adrift, as if he didn't belong here. He imagined a quieter Thanksgiving dinner in East Belfast. It would be Mick, GB and his wife, Deanna, and Maddy. Possibly her cousin would come from Farmington. And they just might ask Velma Cole, who took care of

Maddy when the need arose.

There would be turkey, stuffing, homemade rolls, and fruit salad. "And we will have sweet potatoes," Deanna had said.

"And if one doesn't like sweet potatoes?" Aaron had asked.

"Then one only has to take a tiny spoonful, because a certain little pair of eyes will be watching to see what is done."

Aaron had laughed. "Oh, of course. A good example must be set."

Here in the Walker home, the children, the two younger ones, did not want to settle down. They had fun running up and down the basement stairs, playing tag. Alice had help in the kitchen from her daughter, Courtney, who had arrived the night before. Alice looked flustered. Clearly she wasn't used to such a large gathering either. And Courtney, who didn't know what it was like to be raised with siblings, seemed unable to handle the noise.

"I have a splitting headache!"

Steven came up behind her and rubbed her temples. "Do you want some aspirin?"

"Yes, please."

The baby, Steven Carl, cried then, and Courtney excused herself to go nurse her child. "Mother, can I sit in your bedroom and just close the door?"

"Of course, Sweetie."

When the table was set, with Leighton and Aaron's help, the dinner bell rang. When two of the younger boys didn't come, Leighton rang the bell again.

"This is a special day, a special dinner has been prepared, and we will all sit at these three tables together to partake of this food."

"But, Grandpa—"

"No buts. I'm the oldest person here, and because I am, I get to call the shots. There will be time for playing later.

Now find a chair and sit so I can ask the Lord's blessing on this outstanding meal." He reached for Alice's hand. "Your grandma has worked very hard to fix this for us, and enjoy it we will."

Aaron listened as his father thanked the Lord for the food, the day, the family, the love that filled the room, and then all said, "Amen!"

He liked Alice's dressing, but he couldn't eat more than a couple of bites of anything. He never knew he would miss his friends in Maine so much. It was as if they were his real family, and these were people he barely knew.

He begged off from pumpkin pie, then reached for the telephone. E-mail was fine, but today, especially today, he wanted to call, wanted to hear Deanna's voice and talk a minute to Mick—and to Maddy, of course.

It was quiet when he heard the familiar voice. Of course their meal had long been over.

"Aaron!" She covered the mouthpiece, but he could still hear, "Dad, it's Aaron calling from Oysterville."

After talking to Maddy, he told Deanna that he wanted her to come visit his family. There was a long pause, as if she was deliberating, and then finally she spoke. "Aaron, I'd love to come, but I cannot leave Dad just now."

"Is he still feeling bad?"

"It isn't just that. Who would take over for me?"

"Yeah, okay. You're right."

He hung up, thinking about what she'd said. Was she using her father as an excuse not to come? Perhaps she did not want to see him again. Yet how could he forget the lilt to her voice, the excited sparkle that he knew was dancing in her deep brown eyes as she talked, the way they'd kissed at the airport.

He sat in the office, which so far none of the children had

discovered today, and closed his eyes. He had to decide what course his life was going to take. And he had better decide soon. . . .

twenty-one

"Do you think you'll return to Maine to work at the Lobster Pound again?" Alice asked a few days after Thanksgiving. She'd walked to the bay and sat beside him on the log. He had said very little the two weeks he was home. She knew he'd had one date with an old girlfriend, and though the girl kept calling and he would speak to her, he never went anywhere with her again. She'd known from that first evening, when they'd all been partying and rejoicing at the Portland house where Courtney now lived, that though he seemed happy to be home, his heart was elsewhere.

"Mark my words, Leighton, that boy is not going to be staying," she had said later that night.

"Nonsense," he'd retorted. "He's always wanted to be a crabber, and though I'd like him to work in the store, I'll go along with whatever he wants."

"I don't think he'll stay," Alice said again now. They sat on the deck, enjoying one last day of late fall sunshine. Aaron could be seen through the binoculars where he sat on his log. He was not moving, just sitting still and staring straight ahead.

"Maybe I should walk down and talk to him."

She'd put her hand on his arm. "He'll be up shortly. Let him be. He's thinking it all out."

"If he wants to return to Maine, I think he should do it," Leighton said. "Now that he's come home, we've mended fences; he can go back there. Maybe we'll take a second honeymoon and go meet this Deanna and her daughter."

"Or maybe we should offer to fly her out here."

"No. Can't do that. She's needed there, according to Aaron. Her father isn't well and the brother works, but doesn't help out at the Pound, and that's where the profit comes in."

Alice reached up and pressed a finger along the deep furrow on Leighton's brow. "Then why the worried look? If we're going there, you should be happy about an upcoming trip."

"I'm just not sure yet. Let's wait to see what Aaron decides."

Aaron had trudged back up the trail and to the house in time for six o'clock dinner. He said very little but answered his father's question, saying, yes, a loan would be nice, should he want to buy a crabbing boat, a good used one, and he appreciated the offer.

They discussed other topics, and after Aaron had two helpings of double-fudge ice cream, he said he was going to bed.

Two weeks later, Aaron went to work in the store. He'd helped by setting up strings of Christmas lights for the holidays. He looked forward to hearing from Deanna each evening. Then the letters stopped coming. He sensed something was seriously wrong. He dug out his wallet with the Lobster Pound business card. It was after midnight in Maine, but he knew he wouldn't sleep if he didn't find out.

Nobody answered. He called information for GB's phone number.

A voice answered on the second ring.

"Is this GB's wife?"

"Yes, and who is this?"

"Aaron Walker. I worked at the Pound for awhile."

"Oh, yes. GB talked about you."

"I haven't heard from Deanna and need to know how Mick is doing."

"He's in the hospital, Aaron. GB stayed with him all afternoon, and Deanna is there now. I'll go in the morning."

"What's wrong?"

"Oh, I thought you knew. It's a bleeding ulcer, and he doesn't seem to be responding to treatment."

"What about the Pound?"

"It's closed down. They can't operate it without Mick."

Aaron felt fear for Mick, empathy for Deanna and Maddy. He should be there. They needed him. Even if nothing worked out between him and Deanna, he could do the work; he could scrub floors. They couldn't close the Pound indefinitely. If Mick was worried, that might be the reason he wasn't getting better. He hated hospitals. Aaron could hear him grumbling and complaining now. He needed something to look forward to, to see some hope on the horizon.

He had to go as soon as possible. Now came the part where he told his father.

Leighton and Alice were at the table playing Scrabble.

"Dad, I don't know how to say this or to explain it, but I have to leave. They need me there. In Maine. I just don't know about the money to—"

"Don't worry about the money, Son. Alice said this would happen. I understand, really I do."

Aaron let out a whoop, leaned over and hugged his father, then Alice. He ran down the stairs and packed in five minutes. Alice offered to drive him to Portland to catch the earliest flight out. One left for Bangor at six A.M.

Aaron said good-bye to Hannah's photo, hugged his father again, and followed Alice to the car. He looked out over Willapa Bay; the full moon shone out over the water. He would miss this place, but it wasn't as if he'd never be back. He would have the best of two worlds. God had seen to that.

"Thanks so much for driving me, Alice."

"Consider it an excuse for me to go into town and see that grandson." She smiled, then squeezed his hand. "It's going to work out, Aaron. When you put it all in God's hands, and I think you have, you will be blessed more than you can ever imagine."

They were far too early, but Aaron said he didn't mind waiting, that he'd catch a nap in one of the chairs in the lounge. He kissed Alice's cheek and thanked her again for loving his father. "I have never seen my father so happy. You are good for him, Alice."

"And he is good for me. I didn't realize what I was missing until he came into my life."

"And I leave this time knowing we've made peace and that there are no hard feelings."

"Isn't it a fantastic feeling?"

Aaron thought about that while he sat in the waiting area. Yes, it was a fantastic. He was happy with his life. He had a purpose. He'd never felt committed enough to ask someone to date him exclusively and obviously had never asked anyone to marry him. He was young, after all. A lot of men, and women too, didn't marry this young. He had things to do yet. But try as he might, he couldn't think of what they were. He'd traveled, seen the country, and tried his hand at a host of different jobs. He was back to knowing that the bay was in his blood. It just happened to be a bay on the opposite end of the country.

When the boarding call came, Aaron slung his small backpack over his shoulder and went down the ramp. Deanna didn't know he was coming. He wanted to surprise her. He'd go to the hospital first, see Mick, and let him know he had not deserted them after all, that the Pound would stay open.

He slept off and on most of the way there. They had one layover in Minneapolis, but he didn't bother getting off the plane. It would be late when he arrived, but that was okay. He could find a bus or hitchhike to Belfast.

And if a store was open, he'd find something to take to

Maddy. Being a father would mean doing and being a lot of things, but he felt he was ready for the responsibility.

It was eight when the plane landed. There were just four people getting off, and he and one other passenger were the only ones who were not met by anyone.

"Hey, do you have a ride to wherever you're going? My name's Larry." He held out a hand.

"Aaron." He looked at the man who had sat across from him. "I'm heading to Belfast."

"It's on my way."

"Are you sure? I need to stop at a store, if there's one still open," Aaron said.

The young man smiled. "I know of one. No problem. So you're going to Belfast. I'm just beyond about ten miles."

Aaron mentioned that his boss, Mick, was in the hospital.

"Sounds like you're returning just in time."

Larry chatted while they drove. At a discount store, Aaron found a teddy bear with a red coat and hat for Maddy. He then saw the carnations at the checkout stand and grabbed a bouquet.

Larry dropped Aaron off at the hospital at nine-thirty, and Aaron offered to pay his friend for the ride, but he waved him away. "Like I said, I was going this way anyway. Hope your friend is going to be okay."

"Yeah, me too. Thanks."

Aaron didn't expect to find Deanna still there. She sat in a chair pulled up next to the bed, and his heart pounded at the sight of her holding her father's hand, her head bent. Mick appeared to be asleep; maybe she was too.

He stepped inside. She must have sensed his presence, as she glanced up and let out a squeal as she ran to him, the dark curls bouncing. "Aaron, oh, Aaron. I told Dad you'd come back. He just smiled and said, 'We'll see.'"

He pulled her out into the hall, not wanting to wake Mick. "How is he?"

"He's better; he comes home tomorrow. It's so wonderful to see you."

"You didn't call to tell me your father was in the hospital. I had to call GB's house."

"I didn't see any point in—"

"Why? Because you thought I didn't care anymore?"

Tears began to fill her eyes. "I knew how I felt but didn't dare hope. . ."

Aaron handed her the flowers. "For you. Red. Your favorite color. And I have something in the bag for Maddy. Where is she?"

"At Velma Cole's."

"In good hands, then."

"Aaron, you must be tired. I was getting ready to go home; it isn't as crucial as it was at first. He's going to be fine—just has to follow a better diet. No spices or fats."

He desperately wanted to kiss her, but dare he? He lifted her chin, and their eyes met and held. "Deanna, this isn't the time or the place, but I must tell you. I didn't come back just for Mick."

"Aaron." She shushed his words with her mouth, and he knew then how wonderful it was going to be. God must have had this in mind all along.

"I knew you were the right one after that first day," she said. "I prayed for God to send a soul mate my way. I wanted someone in my life and a father for my daughter."

"I wasn't praying, though."

"That's what's so neat. He answers one person's prayers, and the other one comes to realize that was what he wanted all along too." She glanced in Mick's direction. "I'll tell the nurse I'm leaving and to call me if there's any problems."

They walked hand-in-hand to the car. The rain that had been more mist than true rain had stopped, and a fog now seeped over the area. Deanna glanced up but couldn't see the stars, though she knew they were there. It didn't matter. They'd be out another night.

"Tell me I'm not dreaming," she said, putting her head against his chest. "I don't want this to be a dream."

"It isn't a dream," Aaron said huskily. "It's for real, Honey." He'd never called her "Honey" before, and he liked the way it sounded.

She leaned up and pulled his face down again. "Call me 'Honey' again," she murmured.

"Okay, Honey."

"I like the way it sounds."

"Me too."

"It's a good thing you have the cottage, and I have to stay at the house. . . ."

"You didn't rent out the cottage?"

"What do you mean, rent it out?" Then she saw that he was teasing, and she pulled his cap off and ruffled his hair. "You didn't get a haircut in Oysterville. And you've lost weight."

Aaron hadn't realized it until then. His pants did hang on him. "There are no barbershops in Oysterville."

"What's there, then?"

"A general store, post office, some houses, and a church."

"There must be a barber somewhere."

"Yes, but I decided to let it grow. Do you like it?"

She walked around and looked at the front then the back. "It will do, but if you want to be a backwoodsman, you need to grow a beard."

"I just may do that."

"Just kidding!"

They stood and kissed, holding each other for a long moment

before getting into the car. "This feels good and right."

"Hmmmm," she said in reply. "Next stop is to pick up a sleeping Maddy. I can't wait to see what she does when she sees you."

As they drove, Deanna looked over and grinned. He took out the harmonica and began playing "She'll Be Coming around the Mountain When She Comes."

Deanna's clear alto voice sang the words while he played. "I didn't know you knew how to play a harmonica," she said after five verses.

"I found it in with Hannah's things."

"Oh."

Aaron reached over. "It's okay, Deanna. We'll talk about it sometime. I'm able to tell you now."

She took his arm again, saying nothing.

Velma Cole looked surprised to see the two on her doorstep so late. "The little one is asleep. You could leave her here for the night."

"No way," Deanna said. "I can't wait for her to see Aaron."

"She talked about you a lot," she said, nodding at Aaron. "I'm so happy you came back."

He hugged her and went to pick up the sleeping child.

"Mommy," she began, then opened her eyes. They sprang open, and she screamed out almost the same way her mother had at the hospital earlier, "Aaron!"

The three headed for home, thankful that the fog had lifted.

"The cottage is just as you left it."

"Good."

"You'll be up for breakfast?" she asked as he stood in the doorway.

"You bet."

"Bacon or ham?"

"It doesn't matter. Just give me anything."

As Aaron ran down the steps, Murph followed, as if he wasn't about to let him out of sight again.

"Hey, ol' boy, I missed you too."

This time he let the black lab come with him down the familiar path to the cottage. One day soon he would carry Deanna over the threshold.

epilogue

Aaron would have agreed to elope, as it would mean he would belong to Deanna that much sooner, and she to him. He wanted to make her his wife, but he had to be patient. Mick was recovering; Leighton and Alice had made reservations to come east. Deanna bought a dress and planned a small wedding.

"I don't need a long white dress with veil," she said. "I've been there, done that."

"But Aaron hasn't been married before," Pastor Neal said.

"I don't want a lot of expense," Aaron said. "We can get married by you before God and a few friends and family members and have a reception in the church fellowship hall."

Mick argued the point, though, which Aaron thought was strange. It was women who wanted big affairs, so why was Mick suggesting this now? Then Aaron realized that he had been both mother and father for many years. He was only trying to do what he thought was best.

Six weeks later, on one of the coldest days East Belfast, Maine, had seen in several years, with piles of snow on the ground and more expected by nightfall, Aaron and Deanna would repeat their vows and exchanged rings.

"I love you already," Alice said, as she had agreed to be the matron of honor. "I can hardly wait for you to meet my Courtney."

"And I love Aaron with all my heart," Deanna said. "I never thought I could be this happy."

"Aaron is so settled. He has that look of contentment about him."

Deanna giggled as Alice checked the hem of her dress and made sure the bouquet was in one piece. She leaned over and hugged Maddy.

"I think it's cute that Aaron insisted you walk down the aisle and that your father said Maddy had to be a flower girl and ring bearer."

"And I have the rings right here on this white pillow," Maddy said. "It's so soft, I want to keep it."

"So you shall," said Alice. "I surely can't think of anyone I want to see have it more."

The entourage started: Madison Marie in her lilac gown with tiny rosebuds embroidered in the hem and neckline, then Alice with her dress of a deeper purple, and Deanna with a beige, long dress with scooped neckline and tiny seed pearls that had been carefully sewn in. Pearl buttons went to the waist, and she looked elegant in the straight skirt, carrying white Lily of the Valley and purple violets.

As they repeated their vows, Aaron's hand reached over for his Deanna's. He breathed a prayer to the Lord, who had made this day possible, the Lord who had loved him through it all.

"I now pronounce you man and wife," Pastor Neal said.

"And you get to kiss my mommy, Aaron," Maddy said, looking up with a smile on her face. Laughter sounded from the audience, then someone clapped, followed by another and another.

"And I get to kiss you too," Aaron said, scooping the little girl into his arms and holding his two women close in a tight embrace.

DEANNA'S BANANA WALNUT PANCAKES

2 cups buttermilk
2 eggs, beaten
2 cups flour
1 tsp soda
1 tsp salt

2 tbsp oil
1 cup sliced bananas
    (about 2)
½ cup chopped walnuts

Beat eggs, add buttermilk. Add flour, soda and salt; mix well.
Fold in oil, then bananas and nuts. Drop by ¼ cup measuring cup onto a hot griddle.
Serve hot with real butter and Vermont maple syrup.

A Letter To Our Readers

Dear Reader:

In order that we might better contribute to your reading enjoyment, we would appreciate your taking a few minutes to respond to the following questions. We welcome your comments and read each form and letter we receive. When completed, please return to the following:

Rebecca Germany, Fiction Editor
Heartsong Presents
PO Box 719
Uhrichsville, Ohio 44683

1. Did you enjoy reading *Ring of Hope* by Birdie L. Etchison?
   ❑ Very much! I would like to see more books
      by this author!
   ❑ Moderately. I would have enjoyed it more if
   _____
   _____
   _____

2. Are you a member of **Heartsong Presents**? Yes ❑ No ❑
   If no, where did you purchase this book?_____
   _____

3. How would you rate, on a scale from 1 (poor) to 5 (superior), the cover design?_____

4. On a scale from 1 (poor) to 10 (superior), please rate the following elements.

   _____ Heroine   _____ Plot

   _____ Hero   _____ Inspirational theme

   _____ Setting   _____ Secondary characters

5. These characters were special because _____
   _____
   _____

6. How has this book inspired your life? _____
   _____
   _____

7. What settings would you like to see covered in future
   Heartsong Presents books? _____
   _____
   _____

8. What are some inspirational themes you would like to see
   treated in future books? _____
   _____
   _____

9. Would you be interested in reading other **Heartsong
   Presents** titles?   Yes ❑   No ❑

10. Please check your age range:
    ❑ Under 18   ❑ 18-24   ❑ 25-34
    ❑ 35-45   ❑ 46-55   ❑ Over 55

Name _____

Occupation _____

Address _____

City _____ State _____ Zip _____

Email _____

AS AMERICAN AS APPLE PIE

If it's true that the way to a man's heart is through his stomach, then what better way to entice the typical American male than with apple pie?

As friendship is allowed to ripen and blended with love and grace, a recipe for a wonderful, lasting relationship is formed. When it comes to romance, the sweetest desserts are no match for God's timing.

paperback, 336 pages, 5 ³⁄₁₆" x 8"

❤ ❤ ❤ ❤ ❤ ❤ ❤ ❤ ❤ ❤ ❤ ❤ ❤ ❤ ❤ ❤ ❤

❤ ❤ ❤ ❤ ❤ ❤ ❤ ❤ ❤ ❤ ❤ ❤ ❤ ❤ ❤ ❤ ❤

Hearts♥ng Presents
Love Stories Are Rated G!

That's for godly, gratifying, and of course, great! If you love a thrilling love story but don't appreciate the sordidness of some popular paperback romances, **Heartsong Presents** is for you. In fact, **Heartsong Presents** is the *only inspirational romance book club* featuring love stories where Christian faith is the primary ingredient in a marriage relationship.

Sign up today to receive your first set of four never-before-published Christian romances. Send no money now; you will receive a bill with the first shipment. You may cancel at any time without obligation, and if you aren't completely satisfied with any selection, you may return the books for an immediate refund!

Imagine. . .four new romances every four weeks—two historical, two contemporary—with men and women like you who long to meet the one God has chosen as the love of their lives. . .all for the low price of $9.97 postpaid.

To join, simply complete the coupon below and mail to the address provided. **Heartsong Presents** romances are rated G for another reason: They'll arrive *Godspeed!*

www.heartsongpresents.com
